Tango's face was totally deformed with maniacal rage as he screeched, "Them niggers and that peckerwood done ripped me off!" He turned to the ebonic hood leader. "Boston, we gonna catch 'em and waste 'em. They headed for the Outer Drive back to that peckerwood in the Loop with my hundred grand!"

Alerted to Tango's vengeance, Precious searched frantically for Speedy, Upshaw and the loot, finally spotting them leave the bar and come down the sidewalk with a high yellow stunner between them. "Speedy! Watch it! Run!"

Speedy's eyes were phosphorescent as he halted and stared at Precious for a long moment. Tango's Buick catapulted into the street and Speedy raced into the alley behind Upshaw. The super fox screamed and fled back toward the bar as the Buick roared into the alley in pursuit.

The Buick smashed into Speedy with a terrible crunch sound. He and the valise flew through the air to bowl over Upshaw. Transmission and brakes howled and squealed as Boston repeatedly backed up and shot the Buick's wheels forward over the prostrate targets, crushed and crimsoned on the alley floor.

ONG WHITE CON

D1482382

LONG WHITE CON

ICEBERG SLIM

HOLLOWAY HOUSE PUBLISHING COMPANY
LOS ANGELES, CALIFORNIA

Published by
HOLLOWAY HOUSE PUBLISHING COMPANY
8060 Melrose Avenue, Los Angeles, CA 90046

This Edition Reprinted 2005

This novel is a work of fiction. Names, characters, places and
incidents are either the product of the author's imagination or are
used fictitiously. Any resemblance to actual events or locales or
persons, living or dead, is entirely coincidental.

International Standard Book Number 0-87067-930-9
Printed in the United States of America

PREFACE

I WAS DOZING OFF   early in L.A. to store up energy for a series of college rap gigs I'd be off to in a few days. It was several hours before the fetal Seventies would pop from time's booby-trapped vagina.

I was unaware that fate would, within less than twenty-four hours, pop back into my life the most electric black hustler I'd ever known. How could I know on New Year's Day I'd have a reunion with an unforgettable friend. I mean, Johnny O'Brien, White Folks, the blue-eyed, white-skinned nigger con man from the Big Windy. Dead, black Blue Howard, his spiritual father and mentor, had turned him out on the con.

How could I know White Folks would furnish

5

his account of adventures more gripping and fascinating than his exploits in the novel *TRICK BABY*. How could I, or any black outsider, discover the sacrosanct secrets of the big white con except through White Folks, who played it with a top flight mob.

The phone jangled like the wake-up bells in a cellhouse. I picked up to a silk broad's voice. A chilling sound really, despite the fact that I had expected its owner to contact me. It was Big Apple rotten, glossy and slick as ermine droppings. But how could I know she was tied in to my reunion with White Folks.

"Mister Beck?" she said. "I'm Josephina, the writer. I've arrived, with an inevitable case of jet lag. I'm in Playa Del Rey."

From the sleazed bowels of the ghetto, I replied, "Welcome to emphysema city. I'll present you the key at your convenience. Lady, let's kick off things by dropping the 'Mister' tag."

She faked ingenue flabbergast. "I . . . uh, oh luv! What should I call you?"

I despise phony, pretentious rectums, black and white. I said, "Beck, Bob, Iceberg, Ice, Berg . . . nigger, with love and a smile. Even motherfucker with the light turned down low."

She handcuffed her breath for an instant. You know, like one of those closet bisexual whores in Long Island emoting snob outrage at the visual atrocity of some lackey peasant sneaking a crap in the shrubbery.

She said, "Iceberg, excuse me for a moment."

I heard the dulcet bells of crystal toll as some service person arrived to lay out some booze to cushion her jet lag.

I heard her say, "Thank you very much." Then, to me, "Hi again . . . it's still early, why not come here? To get acquainted . . . get the prerequisite things out of the way, before we put together the actual nuts and bolts of the interview and your profile for the magazine."

I said, "Why not tomorrow night? Even daytime ain't the right time, no time for a nigger to travel across several police division turfs."

"What?"

"I mean, nighttime is never really the time to even walk Fido out to pee. Some roller in heat, with blood lust, might scribble in a death report. Mine! That he thought I was a dead ringer for a mass murderer at large and that the leash was a piece in the dark."

She chuckled oddly, like I was one of the Camarillo Picasso's, in the asylum upstate, who was showing her one of my finger paintings executed in poo-poo on her wall.

She said, "How about tomorrow at noon? Surely you won't need to take precautions then. Mother of Jesus, you're paranoid!"

"All right, I'll see you then. Look, white girl, I wouldn't pull my ride out of the garage until I turned on my hide-out tape recorder to document roller craziness and maybe my murder. If you meet a nigger in these times who ain't paranoid, you've met a nigger dreaming and bucking the odds to die a natural death. Lady, your mag should have arranged a crash course in the black experience before they assigned you to the project!"

She giggled her New York ass off and gave me the address to her pad before she hung up. The jazzy bitch had turned me off before we started.

Now I'm not a supersonic mouthpiece with a law school college course in logic gracing my portfolio. But believe me, sugar babies, I got a Ph.D. in the logical evaluation of ho character. And I sensed that Josephina was a closet ho to her come-blistered diaphragm. I've developed a bloodhound's acuity for smelling out the stench of ho treachery upcoming. And as I indicated, I've assembled the nitro item of paranoia in my survival kit. Understandably, I use that item gingerly. You know, with that twang in the tush care that a herpetologist uses heisting king cobra venom.

I tossed·the New Year in on my bed. I mulled why the prestigious white mag for men had selected a broad, a white broad, to wiggle on the lap of an ex nigger pimp across the several states of his rappings gigs. She was suspect as a cobra all right, I decided as I slipped into Josephina-haunted slumber.

Next day at noon, I found myself sitting with the sensual and curvaceous Josephina, in the posh barroom of her hotel. We sat sipping frosted drinks at a table in a corner of the shadowy joint. We had just put together an agreement to have the first formal interview at my pad in the ghetto next day. After that she would accompany me on the rap tour to flesh out my in-depth profile her mag had commissioned her to write.

We had conned each other that we had a viable bedrock of trust and congeniality necessary for a successful project. But I knew before we boarded a flight in tandem that I was going to find a way to unearth any *sub rosa* motivations behind her saccharine facade. Why the hell *had* they sent a white broad?

She had given me a queasy feeling in the gut with a crack, "Slim, we'll stay loose on the road together. We can just hang out together."

I was double leery when I left her because I knew "hang out" was New York white hippie argot for you know what. Now I'm a fairly well preserved nigger to be at the rim of sixty. But shit, I wasn't Gable. Were her mag bosses shooting for a clay feet expose of the venerable ex flesh peddler? You know, maybe her spermy first person account of what a pedestrian lover I was, despite the mythic scam about my wizard swipe.

Or had the lamb been tethered out to elicit "turn out" action and dialogue from the allegedly reformed monster. What a piece for the mag that would make! Frustrated, what if she framed me? What a fat white slave bit I could catch! Wouldn't that be a rack-up bitch, I thought, as I went through the door toward the parking lot.

We spotted each other at the same instant. White Folks, with luggage, was about to get into a cab near the hotel entrance. We yowled like estranged fairies about to try it again and sprinted into a

9

warm embrace. A knot of white gawkers watched us get into my ride and pull away.

Except for a touch of gray at the temples, he hadn't changed since he had been my cellmate ten years before in 1960. I naturally put him up in my pad. We rapped until midnight about the Big Windy in the old days, and dead Blue Howard. White Folks got sleepy just as he started to run down his adventures with the Vicksburg Kid's big con mob.

Just before we retired, I laid out my deal with Josephina. I ran down to him my reasons why I thought she was a frame-up artist.

His eyes, blue as robin's eggs, twinkled as he stretched and yawned. "Slim, don't worry, we'll put together a document for the lady to sign to test her out. And I might tag along with you on the tour as a white stand-up witness to keep the lady pure in the ticker."

Next day, White Folks and I sat in my living room drinking coffee. We watched the cobra slither into the driveway in a rented compact. She wiggled to the front slammer, appropriately enscaled in a vari-colored mini dress.

I let her in with the classic ghetto grin. You know, coon-shine teeth galore and cold storage eyes. Then I introduced her to White Folks. At the sight of him, her horny eyes veiled over. I noticed her pump fluttering her dress silk down in silicone alley. The bandit odds were ten to five that she'd orgasmed.

She staggered, gap-legged, to the sofa and said

tremulously, "Iceberg! You freaked me out! You were sadistic not to prepare me for Errol Flynn, reincarnated! I feel like a bumpkin, I really do!"

We soothed her by assuring her that Johnny had that effect on the majority of movie buffs he encountered. We rapped minutiae until she leaned toward the coffee table and flipped on her tape recorder. I flipped off the recorder, then slid the unsigned lie detector paper across the table top. She stared at it transfixed, like it was one of her cold-blooded cousins of strike.

I said, "Miss Lady, sign it. Far as the project is concerned, it don't amount to an ounce of snot, really. Just a taste of breast protection for me and my crumb crushers. You know, I'm a squared-up subject from hell. You could flush me and my kids back down the toilet . . . say what if I blew your cool and your sweet human empathy . . . if my chauvinistic bullshit and ego sprung loose on the trip or something. All the paper does, when you Hancock it, is give me the right to delete cut throat shit before you publish it. Sign it, lady, so old Ice can flow and glow with you. You dig where I'm coming from, sugar baby?"

Her porcelain jaw hardened. She grated, "Mister Beck, I can't sign that without authorization."

"I'm certain you've got your boss's home number." I waved toward the phone. "Call him! After laying out long bread to send you three thousand miles, he's a cinch to say 'yeah' to that paper."

She knotted her fists in exasperation as she "jacked in the box" to her feet. She clicked her

11

heels over to White Folks, the two hundred percent nigger. He gazed up at her with bland blue eyes.

She flung her arms out Jolson style and implored him, with piteous "mammy" eyes. "Don't let him do this number on me! Please explain my position to him!"

White Folks shrugged. "What can I do, doll? This matter is over my head. I'm just a nine-to-fiver."

She turned on the waterworks to cop her license to do me in but I was immune to ho tears. I found out why hos cry when I was just a boy. Even poor dead Mama's tears had failed to turn me from that long, fast track. She stood, legs akimbo, fists on hips, chest heaving, a lynching glare beaming down at me. I grinned up at her like Fido juggling a filet.

She blew control. "You fucking nigger wretch!" she hissed as she snatched up her gear.

Now I wasn't, years ago, the refined, defused bomb I am now. I mean, I was ticking! I blew control. I leapt to my feet, maroon eyes bulged out monster style. Maybe I could arrest her ticker with the bit. You know, the perfect murder.

I showered her with spittle as I rammed the doomsday mask into her face. "You come freak snake bitch! Get in the wind before I kick your heart out and stomp on it!"

White Folks stepped between us. She squeezed herself against him and waltzed him to the slammer.

As she stepped through it, she whined, "I'm so grateful for your presence. He would have attacked me!"

12

The chump broad wasn't hip. It was me White Folks was protecting. We watched her Mustang stampede down the driveway into traffic.

As I told you, back then, I was still fresh and jumpy from the street, with a stone age understanding. I was without the rolled steel control and discipline I have now. The sight of an L.A.P.D. cruiser passing in Josephina's wake jolted me to the folly of my wayward passions.

Need I rundown to you the hypothetical horror of the aborted cross? I visualized Josephina, sans White Folks as a witness, of course, butt blood from her noggin against the door frame, rip off her dress and boogie to the middle of the stem screaming that a crazy nigger with a gun had tried to heist her poontang.

I shivered and broke out a fifth of tranquilizer. White Folks and I sat there sipping silently for a long while. He fiddled with and stared thoughtfully at an odd-looking ring on his finger. I vaguely remembered that he wore it when I met him years before in the jail cell back in Chicago.

"That's a pretty ring, Johnny."

He extended his hand and I saw the massive hoop was the cameo likeness of what appeared to be maybe an Inca Indian broad, with the fancy head trappings of royalty.

He said, "Phala . . . Mama was half Indian. She gave it to me the week before she died. It was passed down to Mama from her great, great grandma. Aztec Billy, a Mexican Indian, and grifter whiz, gave it to Grandma. Grandma and Billy were sweet as carnival candy on one another, but Grandma's sod-busting folks wouldn't hold still for a roustabout hustler son-in-law. So Billy and Grandma held hands one day and walked off a cliff together. When I was a little kid I used to bawl when Mama told the tale, and cried almost as hard about Billy's run-down to Grandma, via Mama, about the fate of the Aztec Princess on the ring. Mama said Grandma called it The Unhappy Virgin Ring. So, when the Vicksburg Kid's customers got short in supply for our stocks and bonds set-up in Canada, we put together an irresistible game to take off fat suckers based upon the legend of this ring. It's known in big con circles as the Unhappy Virgin Game."

His eyes became saddened as he paused before he mused on. "The Vicksburg Kid, bless him in his grave, picked up my con education where our dear old friend Blue Howard left off. The Kid knew and kept the secret of my blackness. Soon as I hit Canada he invented for me a cover background and moniker. The Utah Wonder up from the coal pits, he told all the white grifters. I read a ton of books on mining and the coal slaves to protect my cover. He was the first and only white man I've met without a scintilla of racism or bigotry in his heart."

I said, "What a follow-up novel to TRICK BABY that story would make!"

He said, "I agree, but you couldn't use real names of the people involved . . . especially those of the police and politicians. I'm squared up, building a brand new life for myself. I could maybe get hit!

And you couldn't be specific about the locale. You could just refer to it as an area or a city in a southwestern state. And maybe, Slim, you could tell the story in the third person to give it a subtle fictionalized facade. Use your judgment to protect me."

I agreed to his stipulations and we made a financial agreement royalty wise. I set up my tape recorder and for a week White Folks spun out his once in a lifetime tale of his adventures in the heady world of the white long con, and its ultrasonic pace, lush women and scores!

The factual story is White Folks', the closet nigger, told from the point (after leaving Canada) when he roped the seventh mark, in the states, C.P. Stilwell, II, for fleecing against The Unhappy Virgin game. In the interests of vivid delineation of long con game wizard psychology, to afford full reader access to its drama, and for the spectator view of the pulse-slamming scenes and characters of White Folks' story, I have taken one liberty. As he suggested, I have chosen to write his story in the objective third person based upon the facts as he recounted them.

Iceberg Slim

1

THE SOUTHWESTERN SKY was sugary with rock candy stars. The four of them were happy, happy. Life was delicious! White Folks felt the sleek new '62 Eldorado under his hands cruise smoothly as a spaceship through a galaxy of neon. The four of them were Wade "Speedy" Jackson, ex-crack detective and ex-Harlem grifter whiz, his main squeeze, pixie Janie, and Folks' beauteous black Pearl seated beside him. You've made it Johnny O'Brien, he told himself. You've made it to become a big white con roper. Me, a closet nigger expatriate from the black southside of the Big Windy has made it!

A toothy attendant, in a red velvet monkey suit, scrambled to open the doors of the Eldorado.

He drove it away to park. They caught a reflection of themselves, resplendent in dinner attire, mirrored in the glass doors as they stepped into the elegant maw of the supper club.

The room's diners played muted music with the Rogers' silver as the lyrics of their animated chit-chat *sotto voced* politely across the Damask snow of the tablecloths. A strolling violinist teased haunting classics from his fiddle.

Writhing flamelets from candelabras sanctified the diners' faces, ignited their jewels that showered a confetti of congealed fire in the posh haze. A maitre d' from Naples, with a charming appreciation for half "C" notes, seated them grandly at a table reserved for V.I.P.'s.

They had just finished the fourth course of Speedy's birthday supper when she and her entourage walked in. The diners stared at Christina Buckmeister, the coal mines, banking, real estate heiress. Folks thought, she carries herself like the finishing schools and long bread had turned her out, arrogantly, *prima ballerina* gracefully. A lush petticoat snare to the bone.

She paused for a mini instant in passing to her table. He had met her once, casually. Her dog-in-the-manger brother, Trevor, was the Vicksburg Kid's source for the police and bank fixes for Kid's con mob operation.

Christina gave Folks a gray, deliberate blast of she-wolf eyes as she nodded and moved past. Pearl barraged eye gouging vibes when he smiled stingily and nodded back.

He was irritated with himself as he fought to keep his eyes off her even after she had seated herself facing him several tables away. In the cathedral ambience, her flawless patrician features and rosebud mouth shot a lance, half of thrill, half of hatred, through his head. She had a painful resemblance to Camille Costain. He'd never forget that racist assassin of his heart.

He smiled grimly, remembering how his precious white Chicago socialite Goddess had been fatally in love with him before he had confessed he was a nigger that night on Chicago's outer drive at the edge of Lake Michigan. The heartless bitch had cut him loose, crucified his foolish young soul, nearly drowned him, mad and dead, in an ocean of booze to stop the pain that took months to fade away.

The fiddler paused for a moment at his side to break memory's spell with his melodic *Clare De Lune*.

He stared at Christina and wondered if she'd ever visited one of her nightmare coal pits. Wondered if she'd ever heard the pitiful bellow of a black lunger's cough. How he despised that blonde bitch Camille Costain look alike, across the way. He remembered the horror stories he'd read about the coal pit victims of the imperialist, heartless class she symbolized. He fantasized a mob of street bums gang raping her, punching her blue blood guts to ribbons.

But even as he despised her, he felt himself drawn to her. He wanted to garrote her with ropes of come. He was palpitating to despoil her, hurt her, violate her with a hate fuck.

Pearl sneaked a hand beneath the table and pinched his swipe to jolt him from his trance. Pearl said, "Who is that? I'd be thrilled to meet her. Introduce me, Sugar?"

He said, "She's the sister of a business acquaintance . . . there's a rumor she's not thrilled to mix with the common folk."

Pearl persisted, "Well, since you obviously are an exception, couldn't you try for this little Harlem Belle?"

Ebonic Janie piped up, "Yeah Johnny, include this li'l old Central Avenue Fox in, too."

Speedy glared at her and said, "Janie, use your mouth to put some curves on that skinny ass."

Pearl leaned close, begging, "Please, Daddy Sweetback, introduce me . . . who did you say she was?"

He said, "She's Christina Buckmeister. I'll introduce you when we all make the Blue Book and Who's Who."

Janie exclaimed, "Wow! Spee, don't you work for them?"

Speedy said, "Yeah, finish that creamed corn."

The wire thin Vicksburg Kid, and his fluff, junoesque Rita, finally showed to break up the cat game. Since he was late, Folks wondered if the Kid was lugging bad news. They sat down and greeted all around. Kid's tender, brown eyes were placid, so Folks knew the fix and the play for C.P. Stilwell, II, the restauranteur mark, were set in smooth concrete for the next day.

Their waiter was just serving the chocolate

mousse. He gave Kid and Rita menus. Buxom Rita started rattling off a string of calorie loaded items. Kid gently relieved her of the menu and ordered just a salad for them.

Kid said patiently, "Rita, you're on a diet. You've been gobbling booze and junk all day. Trust Pappy to save what's left of what you had that hooked me."

Rita batted her rhinestoned eyelashes seductively like the Vegas chorus pony she once, recently, was. "Please, darlingkins! Let me have a full supper. I promise I won't eat even a bite all day tomorrow to make up."

Kid patted the slight protuberance of her alabaster belly gleaming through her see-through tunic. He resolutely crooned, "Sorry, Big Stuff. Your mouth is a dangerous weapon. I can't let you harm yourself further."

Janie and Pearl, on giggle road, excused themselves for a trek to the powder room.

Before they were out of view, Kid said, "Dove, your nose is reflecting the candelabra. Go fix it."

She snatched a jeweled compact from the sable handbag that matched her wrap and studied her elfin face.

She said, "You need an opthamologist, Pappy Dear."

Kid said, "Then cop a heel and pee."

She muttered an inaudible expletive as she gave him a filthy look and stomped away. Her steepled coiffure glittered like a cache of platinum in the wash of the candelabra glow.

Kid leaned his silver fox head in close to Speedy and Folks. He stage whispered, "Now laddies, there's no cause for undue alarm, but I received some additional research info on that customer we're playing for tomorrow. Stilwell drowned a chum about a fluff when he was sixteen. He's been in the psycho ward of two asylums in the past twenty years. The gent is violence prone! I've alerted the High Ass Marvel, Kate and the shills, so Johnny, we'll have to give him an eggshell play.

"Oh, by the way, Speedy, wire up Victoria Buckmeister's limo, phone and bedroom. Since Trevor has advised me that his mother is cancerous and rapidly losing her mental powers, I want to be privy to any radical business decisions she might make. Especially since Trevor believes the old girl has plans to dump him as Buckmeister Major Domo and place his witch of a sister in charge. I want tapes of every word she utters."

Speedy's hound dog face slackened with awe. He said, "Kid, you and Trevor angled me into the position of Chief of Security for the Buckmeister castle and bank . . . not the old dame's nurse. No one else could get the opportunity and time to bug her bedroom."

Kid patted Speedy's shoulder. "You're bright and creative aren't you, laddie? Find a way and do it within the next forty-eight hours."

Speedy shrugged and grinned. "Sure, Kid. You know me."

They glanced at the girls coming back. They assumed normal postures and made small talk.

They all stayed to keep Kid and Rita company through their salad.

All the way home, Folks couldn't think of anything except C.P. Stilwell, the sizzling mark, and Christina Buckmeister. Pearl's sloe eyes were bright when he slid into bed beside her. He was strung up on a double rack, he thought.

Pearl knew he had been preoccupied since supper. He didn't have to be a mental wizard to bet a nickel against a "C" note she was toying with the suspicion that he was in a fugue from the highbrow shimmer of the Buckmeister broad. He had hurt his woman with his neurotic space-out, he told himself.

He gave her tender, quickie fore pleasure and fast-paced her to a double orgasm to buy some space and time to think about the ways to tighten up his play for the mark. Pearl didn't go to sleep as usual after he had done his number.

Her husky voice was laced with hassle. "Say, Love, I've got a lightweight critique I'd like to give about the trip we just took. Okay?"

He sighed. "Sure, Pearl Delight, but it was a quickie because your old man has a busy day upcoming. I'd like to be sharp and bushy-tailed."

He squeezed her close and kissed her with zest. He whispered, "Now sleep well, puppy pussy. Goodnight Sugarface."

She sat up and said, "Nigger, quickie wasn't it. You were there and yet away somewhere else at the same time. Your jones, the quality of your erection was low, low Daddy, Dear. Where was Mama's baby?"

She was a jealous junkie. He knew he'd have to play to turn her around from her relapse. He didn't answer. He arranged a stricken expression. Then he let his eyes marinate her with pity. She hated that. He put on his pajamas and robe. Her eyes softened. She was chronically ill and she knew it. He'd had a case on Pearl stretching back to Montreal. The case was strongly physical, he decided guiltily. Perhaps her jealousy is forcing me to pity her instead of love her. He was irritated, angry with her for wasting his energy. He needed full energy to play quality con. He turned and made for the doorway.

She said softly, "Johnny, please don't do your split to Speedy's pad across the hall routine. I'm all right now. I'm sorry I did my number on you again. Guess I ain't never gonna kick my you know what. Sure, I've broken boo-koo promises to stop doubting you . . . myself . . . but I'm trying awful hard, Johnny, awful hard. Don't hate me, or leave me 'cause I'm sometimes too dumb and crazy to remember how you feel about me. How I feel about you. Guess my crazy shit is hereditary. Poor Mama blew Papa and the wheels off her happy wagon with the same sad crap."

He said, "You're in the tall, sweet clover with me always, Sugarface. Me and you, darling, nigger tough and crazy against the world."

He went back to bed and held her until her incredibly long and lacy lashes shuttered her eyes in infant slumber. He couldn't sleep. He eased out of bed and soft-shoed to the *chaise longue* on the terrace. Perhaps the lullabyes of the southwest

23

Santa Anas would seduce him to sleep. He closed his eyes and listened to the lilting winds. He heard the erotic screech of a nightbird, the bellicose growl of a cougar.

He remembered the humped-back rats that stood on hindlegs, snarling like midget wolves when he was just a little kid back in the cruel Big Windy . . . the cockroach scouts with E.S.P. . . . the bedbug scouts with Ph.D.'s . . . the piss stink in the kitchen sink pipes, and the decayed blood symbols of mayhem and murder in the hallway . . . the stenches of cancer pus and tubercular spittle that impregnated the very pores of the walls . . . the black kids shooting craps for bottle tops on the stoop . . . .

"I'm Johnny O'Brien, lemme play!"

"Go 'way, Peckerwood. Go 'way 'fore we kill you, Trick Baby motherfucker!"

"I ain't no peckerwood! I swear and cross my heart! I'm a Nigger!"

"*. . . lemme kiss that gorjus little pink prick . . . make you feel so goo-o-o-o-o-ood, darling. Ya round eye gonna wink for some lovin'. . . c'mon, sweetheart, what ya runnin' for? . . . I ain't gonna hurt ya . . . you don't come back here, I'm gonna kill ya next time I ketch ya . . . .*"

. . . steamy July night . . . streetcar stop, waiting for Phala . . . my mom. . . .

"*. . . what's a Trick Baby? am I?*"

"*. . . no, Johnny Angel . . . I was never a bad woman, a whore . . . married your dad, all legal like . . . worked honest since I was ten . . . 'course he was white . . . your spitting image . . . weak, but*

24

he loved us in his own cramped, scared way . . . couldn't stand up to his family trouble and poisons . . . but he loved us, Johnny, don't forget that! Honeybee, this world is really two worlds . . . white first and black last. If your dad had been black, then black kids wouldn't hate you. They'd let you play, 'cause you'd be black like them . . . ."

Remembers his mama stopped slaving in white folk's mansions . . . took a flyer in show biz . . . exotic dancer . . . bucket of blood cabaret, Chicago's southside . . . hustling his shoeshine box down Drexel Boulevard one night, there was Mama! Imprisoned inside the cracked glass case on the concrete front of the bucket of blood sucker trap . . . rhinestone "G" string and the most pitiful smile and sad eyes anybody ever saw. A crooked, monstrous dick, in chalk, below the paper image . . . smashed the glass . . . fists bloodied and hurting . . . he tore his mama's picture into confetti . . . Mama drinking herself into madness . . . Mama . . . nuthouse bench . . . wasted, shin bones shiny in the sunshine . . .

"Mama, it's Johnny, your kid. Mama, please remember me! I've missed you so much, Mama!"

Growling in her throat . . . she giggled like a banshee, rolled her belly like a whore . . . grabbed, leering at his crotch . . . whiny, awful voice . . . "Gimme that dick! Cocksucker. Lemme see it, huh? C'mon, lemme suck it, huh?"

Drunk with sorrow, blinded by a billion tears, he had staggered from her sight.

"Mama! Mama, darling!"

He guessed it was the memories that finally

pummelled him into ragged sleep. He awakened, still on the *chaise,* with Pearl shaking him. The sun was poking golden fingers into his eyelids.

She said, "You had me worried, Johnny. Are you all right?"

He said, "Sure! I feel great. Let's have breakfast!"

After wolfing down hotcakes and bacon, he felt slightly better. He leaned back at the table waiting for her to finish. He remembered he was going to be tied up with the mark for at least forty-eight hours. Perhaps longer. He'd have to be like the mark's Siamese twin after they took him off, until Trevor could move the score, the mark's money, from his Midwestern bank to the Buckmeister bank.

He said, "Darling, I'll be away for a couple of days. Maybe several."

She said, "Oh Hell! There was a movie I wanted to see. Guess I'll solo it. You just got back yesterday."

He said, "I'm sorry, but that's how it goes for a speculator who gets a hot tip on a bargain basement parcel in L.A. Enjoy the flick, baby."

She gave him an odd look and crinkled her tip-tilted nose. "Johnny, how do you operate, viably in real estate, without a license or an office? You had neither in Canada . . . ."

He said, "But Saul did and now has a Nevada brokerage firm."

She said, as she cleared the table, "But Saul never had an office either. You two are something else!"

She kissed him goodbye and he watched her leave to teach elementary school. Pearl loved kids madly. She was teaching elementary school when he'd

26

started with her in Montreal.

At noon, he shaved and showered. He dressed himself impeccably in blue serge Brooks Brothers and ultra fresh linen. He went to the closet and pulled out the two unpacked bags that Stilwell had watched him pack the day before in the downtown suite they had shared for several days. He'd had to take one day away from the worrisome mark for Speedy's party or brainstorm.

Twenty stories down he spotted Speedy, in purple livery, wiping off the rented limo they'd use for the Stilwell play. He called Trevor Buckmeister at his family's bank where he was chief executive. He assured him he'd be ready to be picked up.

The Kid called the instant after he cradled the phone. They had a potentially serious problem. The Stilwell tail had casually mentioned to High Ass Marvel that the mark had a crossed eye. Marvel was spooking rapidly.

He examined his rather haggard face in a mirror. He didn't really feel up to par. But, what the hell, he had no choice except to snort some crystal blow to tango his waltzing energy and leave for his job.

2

SPEEDY DROPPED HIM OFF and rolled away to get some prop papers from the mob's document expert. Kid, in business suit and face tinted American Indian red, let him into plush high rise diggings.

High Pockets Kate, a wizard pickpocket and talented shill, came in on his heels. Aristocratic-looking Kate was costumed in upper crust, high society attire. She sported eye-popping fake diamonds.

The High Ass Marvel, one of the two American Indians playing the big con, arrived shortly after Kate. He was almost a double for the Indian on the buffalo nickel. Marvel was edgy, all right, when the four of them sat down in Kid's redwood paneled den. This was the final briefing before Folks picked up C.P. Stilwell, II, to lug him to the ghost town set-up for fleecing. Kid's Japanese houseboy served cocktails.

Kid leaned back, his five grand choppers decapitated the tip off a Corona Corona. He lit it with a platinum table lighter and blew an aromatic poltergeist of smoke that snake-hipped around the filigreed light fixture in the ceiling.

"Laddies and Lady," he said. "My mild . . . uh, trepidation of last evening about our customer has abated. I feel, excuse the expression, tear-ass ready and fully confident that our ninety grand transaction with Mister Stilwell will conclude without untoward event."

The Marvel, costumed in the tattered regalia of Aztec Billy, the hapless gold slave, pulled at his classic big nose. "Kid, I, ah, well, I've got creepy vibes about the mark. He, ah, well, I'd bet with his funny farm background and all, he brainstorms. And that right eye of his, it's crossed!"

Kid's thin lips shaped an indulgent smile. He tented his delicately boned hands beneath his soft, dimpled chin for a long moment studying Marvel.

Folks knew what the Kid was thinking. The role of Aztec Billy was vital, indispensable to the Stilwell play. There wasn't time to make a viable replacement. Unless Kid could turn Marvel around, he would have to replace Marvel with an untried shill and risk a spotty play for Stilwell.

Kid patted the Marvel's arm and pitched his satin baritone voice sympathetically. "Sure, laddie. You have a solid reason to feel the way you do about

Mister Stilwell's affliction. A partner of yours met an unfortunate end in Baltimore, wasn't it? Back in the late thirties, as I am beginning to recall. Sure-Shot Kid, yes now I do feebly recall the grisly affair."

Marvel cut in, "Sure-Shot and I were lounging around the shed, waiting for the eight-fifteen Super Chief, I think . . . figured we'd cull out, from the lopears arriving, a mark to trim on the "smack." We hooked one, loaded and crosseyed! We flipped coins and busted him out. At the tail end of the blow-off, the sucker drew a hand axe from his waistband, poor Shot lying there, his head hanging from a shred of bloody neck! Dying, kicking, jerking and flopping like a butchered dog. Horrible, just horrible! I vowed I'd never play for another crosseyed mark the longest day I lived. Kid, I'm sorry to put you in a cross like this, but I'm leery of that mark!"

Kid shook his silvered head sadly as he leaned into Marvel's face and whispered, "Listen to a friend whose old enough to be your father. That mark hurt your partner, hurt him fatally. Now you're letting him hurt you, hurt your friends. Don't you see, dear laddie, you have no choice except to play for Mister Stilwell. You owe it to your departed partner. To me, to your profession."

Marvel said, "What?"

Kid crooned, "Laddie, you've got a splendid reputation to protect. Why, when I set up in this town a year ago, I knew I wanted the finest, the most intelligent, the most dependable players available for my store. That's why I selected you, laddie. This is your chance to star against the grain. Don't flee from shadows. Don't let the sucker threat of the lopeared mark that destroyed your partner now destroy your reputation. Laddie, you can't do it! Sure-Shot, in his grave, would frown if you did. If you default here, I will not admire your talents less, love you less. But try as I would, if you panic and default, cop a heel, I couldn't keep it a secret.

"And laddie, I would try mightily, because I've always been inordinately fond of you, son. I could not save you from scorn and rejection by the elite of our profession. Don't you see, laddie, you're much too valuable to squander your energies playing the lousy short con, suffering the cop roustings and head bustings, the chump change scores. No laddie, I won't use the energy and insult your intelligence with a request for your decision. Laddie Boy, if that mark brainstorms, I pledge my life to protect you from harm!"

Marvel just sat there gazing with stricken awe and appreciation for the Kid's velvet turn around pitch before he said, "What the hell can I say, Kid? You're airtight! With a steamroller gee like you playing the inside for Stilwell, I'm in!"

Kid shaped his most charming smile. He patted Marvel's shoulder and purred, "Laddie, I'm so glad you realize that one has to be prepared to be lucky."

Folks sighed relief. Kid caught his eye and winked almost imperceptibly.

High Pockets Kate, the pickpocket whiz and star

player, who looked as much like Eleanor Roosevelt as Eleanor, adjusted her *pince nez* glasses as she got to her feet and faced Kid in mock indignation. She drew herself up and said haughtily, "Saul, sweetheart, I am somewhat unthrilled at the prospect of playing the . . . ah, hazardous Mister Stilwell without the mansion-museum set-up convincer."

Kate paused to lather Folks with an affectionate look of admiration. "The Utah Wonder's performances were wondrously inspired in Canada. He played out so pat his image as the utterly consumed collector of ancient artifacts and memorabilia, his obsession with the Unhappy Virgin Statue and legend."

She sniffed and sighed ecstatically, "Ah, how the mark's eyes would glaze over before they went into trace. Wonder transported them! Saul, I consider it a miserable shame to deprive Mister Stilwell of that marvelously convincing museum."

The grifters laughed at Kate's animated garrulity.

Kid said, "Kate, you've got your gab machine revved up and you're great! Who could tip, sweet Kate, that you're a grade school dropout? I couldn't have done without you for almost forty years. Now friends, I am not happy that for this play, the museum is not set up. But as you all know, we can't set up our splendid props in just a common house. You know it's quite a difficult problem locating a sufficiently remote mansion. Well, I'm glad to report that I am now seriously negotiating for a jewel of a secluded mansion to showcase our Lady, the Unhappy Virgin. All of us feel confident, I'm sure,

32

that the absence of the museum convincer will only be a minimal handicap to the play today."

Kid paused and beamed a proud smile Folks' way before he continued. "The Utah Wonder could tie up Stilwell and play the convincer of the Virgin's legend in an alley or even in a john."

They all laughed.

Kate said, "Saul Honey, of course that's true! I withdraw my complaint. One other thing—will we use the newspaper document to blow off the mark?"

Kid glanced at his watch and stood up to signal the end of the conference. He said, "Katie, I wouldn't play a ding-a-ling like Stilwell without it. Now, let's join the others at the ghost town for the final tightening up before the play."

The doorbell chimed as they all were moving out. It was Speedy. After a flawless run-through of the play, Speedy drove Folks back from the ghost town set up to the city.

Two blocks from the Buckmeister bank, Speedy got out from under the wheel of the limo. He went into a fast food joint. What a flap if one of the bank guards saw Speedy, their chief, in purple livery, Folks thought.

He got under the wheel and drove to park in front of the bank. The brass Buckmeister coat of arms gleamed on the black marble facade. A steady flow of the bank's clients entered and exited. He saw a battery of tellers servicing lines of clients in the bustling interior vastness.

He hit a blow of crystal dust behind his handkerchief. He lit a cigarette and waited for Trevor to show. After several minutes, he got restless. He stepped out to the sidewalk to window shop a swank boutique for fluffs adjacent to the bank. The corner of his eye snared Christina Buckmeister alighting from her pink Excalibur a bit down the stem.

He glued his eyes to the jewelry display mirror inside the boutique window and studied Christina. She was gazing his way, still-lifed on the sidewalk like a statue of Aphrodite in heat. Her long tapered fingers were frozen on the swung out door of the Excalibur. He could almost hear her ticker booming as it sprinted against his own. She has the incandescent hots for me all right, he decided. She slammed the Excalibur door and pranced his way.

As she passed, her contralto voice and Paris Lilac rode back on April zephyrs, "Good afternoon, Mister O'Brien."

He turned his head her way and sent on return winds an indifferent, "Good afternoon to you, Miss Buckmeister."

He turned his eyes back to an exquisite jade necklace that he visualized caressing Pearl's plum-hued throat. Satan's voice rattled him as it encored, purring mockingly at his side.

"Mister O'Brien, forgive me if I've startled you, but I couldn't help noticing on passing that you appear as famished as I am. I've ordered a bountiful late lunch from Antoine's and I should be delighted to share bread with you . . . and show you our fabulous bank."

Their eyes duelled in the display mirror for what

seemed like eons. His cocaine arid throat was paralyzed. Steamy time suspended. His tongue flicked irrigation across his parched lips.

He croaked to her reflection, "Thanks, but I've had a late lunch."

She tossed her head to flop an errant forelock from her eyes. The sun exploded golden Roman candles from her mane of spun silk hair.

Irritation laced her voice. "Then I insist that you have an after lunch cocktail."

He felt like a lopeared mark sensing from the sultry amusement in her hooded orbs that she knew she was shaking him up. He'd have to turn and face her, he thought, seize control of the situation with his usual refrigerated composure. But he was afraid she'd tip to his hatred, to his pulse flogging desire.

Trevor's voice cut him loose from her rack. "Chris! Johnny!"

They turned to face him. Trevor glanced at his wristwatch. His blue eyes twinkled knowingly. "Johnny, I'm sorry to be late. Shouldn't we be getting along?"

She said, "I've been holding Mister O'Brien hostage for cocktails. Now, as usual, you've spoiled the fun."

She just stared up into his eyes as he held her extended hand. Trevor cleared his throat. They disengaged.

She said, "Bye until the next time, Mister O'Brien."

He replied, "Until next time Miss Buckmeister."

She turned and whipped her Grable props down the sidewalk into the bank. Trevor and he went to the limo and pulled it away to pick up Speedy. On their way to the suite Folks shared with the mark, Speedy pulled into the far corner of a sprawling supermarket parking lot.

Folks disguised himself as millionaire artifacts freak Alex Remington, as Stilwell knew him. He covered his blond hair with a curly black wig. He camouflaged his blue eyes with dark brown contact lenses.

Trevor disguised his youthfully handsome face with heavy horn-rimmed glasses, a gray wig and appropriate wrinkles with materials from his banker's briefcase. He would play the rather minor but exacting role of Folks' business manager and curator of artifacts and other prizes of antiquity.

Since they had privacy on the back seat with a glass partition between Speedy and themselves, Folks decided to ask Trevor a personal question. He had been aching to ask the question ever since Kid and himself had yielded to Trevor's persistent requests to learn and play the big con.

Finished with his transformation, Trevor asked, "Well Johnny, critique me."

Folks said, "Trevor, you're a makeup magician. Even your sister, at face to face range, couldn't know you."

As Speedy tooled the limo from the lot, Folks said softly, "Sport, forgive me for asking, but I'm curious to know why a splendid legit gentleman like yourself, with the world smooching your keister, yens to hang it out playing the con and risking the penitentiary?"

His haunted, aristocratic face became radiant with visceral passion. His voice tripped and staggered the precipice of nude emotion, "I have, since I was an innocent child, abhorred the slavish regimentation forced upon me by the Buckmeister name and status garbage conventions. I despise the hypocrisy of my immoral peers, with feet of shit, who parade like Gods of Olympus, with total immunity to justice, on this earth.

"I hunger for the rapture of extreme risk, for the so-called criminal big con that promises no immunity . . . nothing! . . . except the most transcendent transport of ecstasy. As a child, my empathy always throbbed for the spider, not the fly. At the circus, I rooted and thrilled for the tiger, not the trainer. Please Johnny, don't stop teaching me into your secret world. Indenture me in your world, nourish my starved soul in your world, don't let me perish in Mother's and Christina's world."

Folks embraced him and said, "Trevor, you'll always have sanctuary with us. You are forever welcome, my dear comrade, as friend and colleague."

They made a fast stop at the mob's warehouse and coupled a trailer to the limo that was loaded with a canvas-covered portable fluoroscope.

Speedy reached the downtown hotel around four p.m. Folks and the bellman, with his bags, went through the lobby to the elevators. Trevor stayed with Speedy in the limo until his cue was due to join Folks and the mark in the suite. As

Folks rang the suite doorbell, he glanced into the half opened door of the room across the hall. Two grifter tails, keeping round-the-clock tabs on the mark during Folks' one day hiatus, looked up from a hand of Gin. They gave him the A-OK office that the mark was still on stable playing ice.

He heard Stilwell's elephantine thirteens stomping the carpet to the door. He slipped on a mask of disappointed gloom. The mark swung the door open. His moon face lit up like Macy's Christmas tree. He slugged a ham hock hand against Folks' shoulder and snatched his bags from the aggravated bellman. Folks restored his neon smile with a ten spot.

Folks shut the door and followed his bags into his bedroom. It was indecent the way Stilwell looked at him, he thought. He was so happy to see Folks, like he was a beloved son he hadn't seen for years. Well, Folks thought, the first lesson I learned from Blue Howard was the art of the rapid artificial aging process of friendship in the mark's heart and head.

Folks sighed and collapsed on the side of the bed. The mark crashed down beside him, a concerned paternal expression creased his freckled forehead.

He said, "Gawd, my boy, you look torn down. It was a wild goose chase, wasn't it? You didn't find that piece you've got your heart set on?"

Folks closed his eyes and massaged his eyelids with his finger tips. He murmured, "No Cecil, I didn't. Maybe the statue existed only in the scuttlebutt of ancient drunkards. I've spent ten years and a fortune, turned two continents inside out searching for her. Oh God, where can she be? If she exists! I was certain I'd find her here in this area."

The mark tugged at Folks' sleeve and said, "Let me fix a drink and order some food."

He slipped off Folks' jacket and stooped to pull off his shoes. Folks looked down at his sympathetic, seamed face. He didn't look like a murderer at all, Folks thought, as he followed him to the mahogany bar. He shook up a series of double martinis and ordered food then sat at the bar beside Folks, comforting him for a couple of hours.

Folks strolled into his bedroom and closed the window drapes to cue Trevor. He went back to the bar and waited for the desk to announce Trevor. He let Stilwell pick up the desk ring several moments later. He looked at Folks with his mouth agape as he passed him the receiver.

Folks said, "Yes, this is Mister Remington. Who? Mister Lee! My business manager, why, I can't believe it! Put him on!"

Trevor came on.

He said, "Mister Lee, what the hell are you doing in town? This morning I sent you to Indiana to evaluate Mister Stilwell's parcel of farmland for purchase. You're fired! What? You're certain of that? Let me speak to the desk clerk. All right, Miss. He's my Mister Lee, pass him."

He hung up with a shocked face.

He whispered, "He claims he's found her! The Unhappy Virgin Statue here in a ghost town. If he hasn't, I will draw and quarter him!"

Shortly the doorbell chimed. He opened the door to Trevor. Exultant Trevor seized them both when he opened the door. He danced them into the living room, gurgling with wanton joy, then pulled them down on the sofa beside him.

Folks said, "Now control yourself, Mister Lee, and give me a coherent report of your alleged find."

He babbled, "Alleged in a pig's eye! I've found her an hour's drive away . . . ghost town . . . a derelict called Aztec Billy, oblivious to her fame and glory . . . the fool has junked the statue behind his shack."

Folks said evenly, "Mister Lee, have you ascertained her authenticity? Are you sure she isn't an excellent reproduction?"

Trevor exclaimed, "She's the Virgin! I've seen her! I've verified five points of her authenticity and I tell you, Mister Remington, she's real!"

Folks shook his head dubiously. The mark, between them, swiveled his head in the crossfire con, like a tennis buff at the Forest Hills championships.

Folks said, "Five points verification isn't enough. I need ten, and that requires our fluoroscope, which, unfortunately, is in the field in New Mexico."

Trevor leapt to his feet, his face smug. He proudly drew himself up and said, "You have an efficient, inventive man in your employ, Mister Remington. I rented a fluoroscope a half hour ago for immediate confirmation of the statue's authenticity. Albert, your chauffeur, and I have it hitched to your limousine out front. Well, what are you waiting for,

Mister Remington?"

Folks said, "A fluoroscope couldn't prove ten points with daylight gone."

Trevor laughed. "That one on the street can. It's one of the latest, with an ultra violet capability."

Folks let the floodgates of ecstatic joy burst free. He leapt up and hugged Trevor. He jigged and raced to the bedroom for his jacket and shoes. He sprinted through the open door behind Trevor, and heard the mark pounding the carpet behind him.

As Speedy cruised from the city limits, Folks lay his head back on the cushions between Trevor and the mark.

He mused the "convincer" legend of The Unhappy Virgin. "Ah, what a poignant legend she bears, my magnificent obsession. What a bitter, awful story her living counterpart suffered ages ago.

"Once upon an incestuous time, an Aztec King fell madly in love with his voluptuous virgin daughter. The King was determined to be her first lover. One night he stripped nude and invaded her chambers. He carressed all the secret, fragrant places with his eager tongue. But she awakened and she clawed and maimed the King. The royal guards rushed to his rescue. They raised their daggers to slay her, but the King saved her for a worse, hellish fate. Jail . . . until she agreed to lavish her royal cherry on the King.

"He imprisoned her in a tower in rags, and on her sixteenth birthday, the King decided to make any hankie pankie impossible. He gifted her with a bigger than life size gem-encrusted statue in her gorgeous image. The jewels were worth millions, but the interior of the statue was a spy post. A succession of slaves were imprisoned inside the statue, each fed and watered until death. And in that bleak tower the Unhappy Virgin became old, ugly and dead!"

The mark said, "I know that freakish King is turning on the spits in hellfire. Mister Lee, I don't suppose the statue is still wearing her jewelry?"

Trevor said, "Unfortunately not, Mister Stilwell. They were most likely removed by the King at the Unhappy Virgin's death."

Speedy maneuvered the limo through the heavy traffic of a main highway. He turned into and moved slowly down a rutted road into the mouth of the bleak main street of a ghost town. Mountains loomed in the background. A ghostly double row of derelict shacks lined the main street. They crouched like battered vultures in the eerie twilight. A coyote was silhouetted on a rise as he raised his muzzle and howled.

In the rear view mirror, Folks got a glimpse of the prop decaled state police car, driven by two grifters in uniform, turn in behind them. They snuffed the cruiser's lights and pulled it into concealment. The limo glided toward a flickering glow of lantern light splashing from a lopsided shack at the end of the street. Speedy pulled up in front of the shack. The head and shoulders of the statue loomed up above the shack at the rear.

Folks said, "Mister Lee, you and Albert set up that machine immediately to check out the statue's

42

authenticity."

Speedy leapt out and opened the limo doors. Stilwell and Folks got out and Speedy pulled the limo to the rear of the shack. The Kid, in a dove gray suit, wore a beaded headband to control his long coarse black wig. Kate and a grifter detective stood beside Kid, gazing sadly down at Marvel lying on a straw mattress on the rough pine floor, apparently in a coma. Marvel, in tattered underwear, was skillfully made up as a torture victim with cigarette burns and bruises.

Suddenly Marvel opened his blank eyes. He clutched Kid's hand in a death grip as he walled up his eyes.

Marvel croaked, "Jimmy, thank God you're here . . . dear Brother . . . horrible, Jimmy! They tortured me . . . to steal my millions . . . all yours, Jimmy. Wouldn't tell those lice where . . . ."

The grifter detective leaned down close to Marvel and said, "I'm Detective Ware. They, the bandits, did you know them?"

Marvel gasped and death rattled. He fell back, apparently dead. The detective tucked Marvel's limp hands across his chest and pulled the flour sack sheet over his face. Then he took out a report notebook and pen.

Kid's face was tragic with sorrow. He said, "Poor dreamer, Billy. Treasure slave! Bled his sweat all over the world for twenty years, dreamed here . . . uranium, big strike here . . . murdered here!"

Kid choked up as the detective scribbled furiously in his report book.

He said, "Be careful! Don't touch anything as we move out of here."

The detective picked up the lamp. The mark was in a trance as Folks took his arm to guide him toward the door. The cop steered them from the shack before he followed. He stooped down beside the shack and they all gathered around him as he very carefully retrieved a fancy gold lighter. He cradled the lighter in his palm as he showed it to the con mob.

He swept his cold cop eyes across their faces and said, "Any of you folks lose this item?"

They did not respond. He carefully sealed the lighter in an envelope and pocketed it. Then he took his pad and pen in hand to jot down names. Kid tugged at his sleeve. The cop turned and faced him.

Kid said, "Detective Ware, is there any chance that lighter could lead to Billy's killers?"

The cop pulled at his earlobe and said, "Possibly. Perhaps the lab can lift prints. The lighter was apparently purchased at Cartier's, that famous jewelry firm in New York City. Now, Mr. Dancing Rain, tell me everything you know about those millions in cash the killers believed were here."

Kid said, "I can assure you, Detective Ware, that those millions in cash existed only in Billy's delirium. Apparently the rumors about that damn legend of the Unhappy Virgin Statue Billy dug up prospecting for gold in Mexico, years ago, sent those murderers here."

The cop said, "Rumors? A legend about a statue sent the killers?"

Kid said, "The legend was, an Aztec King had

the statue sculpted in his daughter's image, encrusted with priceless gems. The false rumors were that Billy peddled the stones for millions in cash. Look, Detective Ware, only a pauper or a lunatic miser would stay in this lonely hole for twenty years! Billy was broke!"

The cop sucked his teeth and said, "Apparently, Mr. Dancing Rain, just apparently."

Kid screwed up his face in surprise. "What?"

The cop said, "It happens to be an official fact that some people allow themselves to die in terrible poverty while in possession of fortunes."

Kid waved his arms in exasperation. "I know Billy was broke!"

The cop glanced toward a wooded section on a nearby rise. He said, "Maybe. Nobody enter that shack while I look around. I'm holding you responsible, Mr. Dancing Rain."

He got into a Chevy and drove toward the rise.

Folks said, "Mr. Dancing Rain, you have my . . . our warmest sympathy. I hope it is not, uh, indelicate to inquire as to when and how you plan to dispose of your brother's property?"

Kid said, "Mr. Remington, I am aware that only intence interest could have brought you and Mrs. Osborn such long distances. As Billy's only surviving heir and administrator, I am prepared to sell everything now, at auction. The proceeds will be the reward offered to send Billy's killers to the death house. Are you a prospective bidder, Mister Lee?"

Trevor said, "Thanks for the invitation, Mr. Dancing Rain, but I think not."

Kid turned to Stilwell and said, "And you, Mister Stilwell, do you plan to bid?"

Stilwell said, "No, I don't think so, sir. I, too, am on the selling end. I am just with Mr. Remington. He is interested in a parcel of Indiana farmland I own."

Kid said, "Good for you, Mister Stilwell."

Then Kid turned to Kate and Folks. He said, "Mrs. Osbourne, Mister Remington, shall we go to the stable and to the relics next door?"

Trevor came to Folks' side. The mark moved in close. Trevor leaned in close and stage whispered into Folks' ear. "She's real! Fifteen points of authenticity!"

Folks said, "Mister Dancing Rain, Mister Lee, my business manager and curator of artifacts, has refined my interests to a solitary piece. The Indian Maiden Statue at the rear of your late brother's sha . . . uh, home."

Kid snorted and said testily, "I am very sorry, Mister Remington, that I can not satisfy your, ah, limited interest. My time is much too valuable to auction piece by piece. That could take days. Highest bidder takes land and all."

Folks said, "Mister Dancing Rain, please excuse Mister Lee and me for a moment."

Kid said, "Of course. I'm taking Mrs. Osbourne to the stable."

Kid and Kate went into the stable-curio shop, which was flush against the shack. Stilwell, Trevor and Folks stood outside the darkened death shack in the glow of bright stars.

Folks stage whispered, as Stilwell moved his ears in close. "Mister Lee, this is an extremely unfortunate turn of events. However, I am prepared to bid for Mister Dancing Rain's whole package. I must have that statue!"

Trevor and Folks moved quickly from the mark toward the lamplit stable. The mark halted when he heard Marvel moan. He turned and went into the death shack when Marvel cried out, "Jimmy! My millions are . . . ."

Folks went to a peep hole in the stable wall, which was also a wall of the death shack. He watched the mark strike a match in the blackness of the death shack. In the feeble flare of flame, he saw the mark as he leaned down close to Marvel's sheeted face. A moan issued from beneath the sheet. The mark uncovered Marvel's face. Marvel's eyes fluttered open and stared up blankly. The mark put his ear close to Marvel's mouth.

Marvel whispered raggedly, "Jimmy? . . ."

The mark's *basso profundo* voice cracked as he tried to fake the Kid's higher register voice. "Yes Billy! It's me, Jimmy!"

Marvel sighed. "Get out my millions, Jimmy. Duffel bags . . . ."

The mark said, "Billy, where?"

Marvel gasped, "Don't let the gov'ment steal it! Get it out!"

The mark pleaded. "Sure, Billy. Where? where, Billy?"

Marvel moaned as he quivered uncontrollably. He closed his eyes as he sighed out his last line of the play. "Aztec Virgin . . .'neath her feet."

Marvel went limp. The mark's match burnt out. Folks saw his shadow dash from the shack. He went to a rear wall to a stable peep hole. He watched the mark race to the ten foot statue at the rear of the shack. The mark struck a match. The portable fluoroscope gleamed beside the statue. He aimed it downward and put his eye against the machine's eye-piece.

Folks knew he was looking at fat, bulging canvas duffel bags buried in a large hole in the earth beneath the statue's feet. The tops of several of the bags were gaped open, exposing prop bales of play money, topped off with real paper money. The mark fled the statue. Folks turned back to the play in the stable, packed from floor to ceiling with dusty bric-a-brac and statuary of many sizes. He took his position with Kate, before Kid. Kid struck a tomahawk against an old horseshoe. The excited mark rushed into the stable.

The Kid said, "Mrs. Osbourne bids forty-five thousand . . . once!"

He tomahawked the horseshoe.

He intoned, "Forty-five thousand . . . twice!"

The mark moved up front. His face was suffused with larceny.

The mark shouted, "Mister Dancing Rain, I would like to join the bidding!"

Kid glanced inquiringly at Folks and Kate. They shrugged assent.

Kid said, "You're welcome to join us, Mister Stilwell. I'm bid forty-five thousand twice!"

The mark said stoutly, "Mister Dancing Rain, I

bid fifty thousand!"

Folks said, "I bid sixty thousand."

The mark's ear wiggled as Trevor stage whispered into Folks' ear. "Now remember, Mister Remington, past eighty-five or eighty-seven thousand, which is your liquid capital at the moment, you will have lost the legal capacity to bid here under Mister Dancing Rain's rules of auction. Two days hence your liquid capital will be four million after the sale of that Australian property."

Folks said, "Mister Lee, have you lost your mind? Arrange a remedy for me with Mister Dancing Rain. I'll liquidate a million dollars of my holdings immediately if necessary. I need a time break. Damn it, man! Can't you understand? I must have that statue!"

Trevor was about to make Folks' request of Kid when the mark piped up, "Mister Dancing Rain, I would like to request a moment's suspension in the bidding."

Kid studied him for a moment before he said, "All right Mister Stilwell. Take five minutes."

The mark's big buck lust had him racked up, Folks thought. He pulled Folks and Trevor to the side. He took a pen and pad from his coat pocket. He rapidly scribbled an agreement that the statue was Folks' for one dollar. He signed it.

He whispered, "Now, friend, give me a dollar. The statue is yours if you drop out of the bidding."

Trevor and Folks looked at each other with genuine astonishment that the mark was playing himself.

Then Folks bit his lip doubtfully. He said, "Mister Lee, can I acquire title to that statue in this . . . informal manner?"

He said, "Why not, Mister Remington? I'm a notary."

Trevor gave the mark a dollar and took the paper.

Trevor said, "That was a noble gesture, Mister Stilwell. But something puzzles me. Why your sudden interest in this ghost town and its rather tawdry assets? The statue excluded, of course."

The mark said, "I guess I discovered a compelling charm and mystique about this place."

Kate shouted, "Mister Dancing Rain, Mister Stilwell's five minutes have expired. I bid seventy thousand!"

The mark said, "Seventy-five!"

Kate bid, "Eighty!"

The mark bid, "Eighty-five!"

Kate took out a sheaf of prop checks and currency. She examined the boodle with a worried face.

She said weakly, "I bid eighty-nine "

Stilwell beamed and shouted, "I bid ninety thousand!"

Kate turned away disconsolately.

Kid banged the horseshoe and waved a deed. "Once, twice, thrice. The ghost town and its goods are yours for ninety thousand dollars, Mister Stilwell . . . if you have that purchase price in cash or its equivalent."

Stilwell snatched out a billfold. He waved a check and a sheaf of currency. He said, "I have here, Mis-

50

ter Dancing Rain, my certified instrument for seventy-five thousand. I'll make it payable to you. I also have an additional fifteen thousand in cash."

Kid said, "All right Mister Stilwell. Step up here and get your bill of sale and we'll set the other papers of transfer into motion."

Trevor, Kate and Folks left the stable. Instantly, they were drowned in blinding light. The two uniformed grifter troopers pulled up before the stable and switched off the spotlight. They got out and pretended to chat with the mob. Shortly, Kid and the mark came from the stable.

One of the troopers said to Kid, "Mister Dancing Rain, we contacted that physician. An ambulance should arrive any moment."

Kid said, "Thank you very much, but it's too late. Billy passed away."

The trooper said, "Mike, get on the horn and get a coroner's wagon out here."

His partner went to the cruiser.

Folks said to the mark, "Congratulations, Cecil, and thanks for your generosity to me."

He said, "I'm very fond of you, Alex."

3

FOLKS SAID TO TREVOR, "Well, Mister Lee, let's pack in the fluoroscope and get back to the city. I'll have a truck sent out here first thing in the morning to get my lady."

Two hours later they assembled in the hotel suite. The mark was jumpy as hell, and obviously eager for the others to leave. The mark compulsively glanced at his wristwatch as he yawned elaborately.

Folks visualized the scene at that moment at the ghost town. The grifter troopers, the fake detective and Marvel had removed the state police decals from the cruiser. They had loaded the Chevy and cruiser with the prop fortune crammed into the duffel bags and were on their way back to the city.

The mark frowned as he studied the dial of his

watch. Kid ran an index finger down the crease in his trousers to signal split time. Kate rose and stifled a yawn.

She said, "Thank you, Mister Stilwell, for a pleasant time."

She walked over to the mark as Kid got to feet.

Kate smiled into the mark's face. She said, "I think you're such a lovable man, Cecil, despite your winning bid for that lovely ghost town."

The mark took Kate's hand and pressed the back of it against his cheek. He said, "My dear, now I am sincerely sorry I bid you out. I have your card, if and when I decide to sell that ghost town, and you shall be the first notified."

She said, "Thank you, Cecil."

She shook his hand and moved away for the door. Kid shook Stilwell's hand and followed Kate from the suite. Folks rose to his feet and stretched himself drowsily.

He said, "Cecil, I'm bushed. Goodnight."

Stilwell said, "Sleep well, Alex."

Folks went toward his bedroom, and Stilwell suddenly stopped him.

He said, "Alex, may I have a moment?"

Folks read the greed in his eyes as he turned to face him.

He said, "Alex, I, uh, well, our deal for that parcel. When will your Mister Lee get to Indiana to appraise it?"

Folks smiled as he extracted a packet of mail from his jacket pocket. The mark had seen him pick up his mail at the desk on their way up from the ghost town. What he didn't know was that Kid had sent the packet, including a crisp fake telegram. Folks removed the telegram from the envelope and extended it to Stilwell.

He said, "Cecil, read this."

Stilwell took it, and stared down at it. A broad smile blossomed on his face.

He chortled, "You're a sly one, bless your heart! Mister Lee has already left for Indiana to evaluate and expedite our deal. What a beautiful meeting of minds!"

He seized Folks in a warm embrace. Then Folks went into his bedroom thinking the mark's greed made him deserve everything he was getting. After all, he intended to shaft Folks for four times the fair market value of his white elephant parcel of land.

Two hours later, Folks heard the mark stirring. He peeped through the key hole and saw that he was fully dressed at the front door. He had a furtive, excited look on his face in the half dark. He very carefully opened the door, eased himself through the door and very quietly pulled it shut.

Folks picked up the bedroom phone and called the tailers across the hall. One of them picked up. He told him to call in a report on the mark's actions as frequently as was possible. Fifteen minutes later, Kid called. They could predict the mark's thinking at this point, so they planned the choreography of the mark's blow-off in some detail.

Forty-five minutes later one of the tailers called in. He said, "I went in on foot to eye that egg. He came in with a camper he'd rented and a brand new shovel. You would've busted your guts laughing at that lopear when he dug down to nothing. He just stood there beaming a flashlight into the empty hole. Then he screamed like his putz was in a vise. He almost wrecked the camper coming out and he gave a couple of trooper cruisers the twice over coming in, just like he should. He's convinced our troopers burned him for the stash. He's on his way downtown in a cab. Sweet blow-off! Toodle-oo, Wonder."

Shortly, the mark showed back. Folks heard him anguishing about. Folks went into a deep slumber bit when he heard him approach his door. The mark eased it open and just stood there. Christ! this is eerie, Folks thought. And dangerous! I know that a guy with his documented malice, under stress, could brainstorm and try to do me maximal harm if the tumblers of the swindle accidently clicked into place inside his head. I couldn't really win a death bout with him. Say I managed to kill him, my purse would be the death house. But the mark shut the door.

Folks soundlessly locked the door. He had selected the suite in a wing of the hotel that gave visual access to the lobby. He put high-powered binoculars to his eyes and saw Kid sitting casually, smoking a cigarette in the moderately crowded lobby. He was gazing across the lobby through a window at the early morning crunch of workers scampering to their jobs.

A morning newspaper delivery truck pulled to

the curb outside the hotel. The delivery man leapt from the cab of the truck with a bundle of papers, then went to the concession stand. He placed his bundle of newspapers into a rack adjacent to the concession stand, then carried a surplus of three newspapers away under his arm as he came across the lobby on his way to the exit.

Kid snapped his fingers at the passing delivery man. The delivery man rolled one of the papers quickly as he turned and took the paper to Kid in exchange for a coin, then turned away. Kid spread the legitimate newspaper across his knees. Folks watched Kid take their prop newspaper from his coat pocket.

Then his binoculars followed Kid as he flung the legit newspaper into a trash can. He moved across the lobby and went to the newspaper rack at the concession stand. A young female clerk smiled at him behind the counter as Kid plucked several cigars from a box. At the same time, his other hand slipped the prop newspaper into the newspaper rack atop the pile. Then Kid placed money on the counter. He turned his head and snapped his fingers.

A bellboy came to Kid's side beside the newspaper rack. Kid pulled his prop newspaper from the rack and folded the headlines inside. Then he snapped a rubber band about the rolled paper, gave it, and a dollar bill to the bellboy. Kid purchased all the morning newspapers and went through the front door. He was going to shred them and dump them into an alley trash bin.

The blow-off was in motion! Folks waited to

hear the doorbell chime. Five minutes later, he heard the chimes. He cracked the door as the mark opened the front door.

The bellboy said, "Mister Remington's morning paper, sir."

The mark took the paper and slammed the door in his face. He opened the newspaper and scrutinized it as Folks eyed him from his bed. The mark came toward him and sat on the side of the bed. Folks shifted so his face was turned away. His breathing was heavy and deep as he faked sleep. He shook Folks' shoulder and Folks stirred and groaned. He turned, with cloudy eyes, to face the mark.

He said, "What's going on, Cecil?"

Cecil spread out the newspaper on the bed. Folks propped himself up on an elbow as he studied the front page.

He read aloud, "*State troopers quizzed in theft of ghost town millions . . . ten millions recovered in ravine. Troopers blame a mysterious nocturnal group for theft of secret hoard. Murdered Aztec Billy is suspected of the multiple murders of mining cronies during the past thirty years in Mexico and in Nevada. Robbery is theorized as the motive for the series of homicide.*"

Then, he paused to read the bold print of a related item. "*At his interrogation, fifteen thousand dollars in cash was confiscated from Jimmy Dancing Rain, brother of deceased Aztec Billy, by Treasury Department agents.*"

Cecil snarled, "Those rotten, crooked state police! I could kill them!"

57

Folks leapt to his feet. He went to the closet and pulled out his bags. He started to speed dress as the mark stared at him with jaws loose.

He said, "Alex! What on earth are you doing?"

Folks said, "Going home! I've got a respectable reputation and family to protect. You can be certain, Cecil, the government is going to root out and smear everybody's name connected to those millions of dollars and a murder victim!"

Cecil sat on the edge of the bed with a shocked look on his face as he removed the phony quit claim deed and bill of sale for Kid's set-up ghost town. He balled up and crushed the documents in his fists.

He said, "I better call today and stop payment on that check I gave Jimmy for the ghost town."

Folks rushed to face him. He said, "Cecil! Compose yourself! You can't stop payment on a check for seventy-five thousand dollars without drawing dangerous attention. Furthermore, you're mangling your ninety-thousand-dollar receipt."

Cecil opened his fists and stared at the crumpled documents in his palm. He said, "You really think Jimmy Dancing Rain would refund my ninety thousand . . . with all this trouble?"

Folks took the documents. He ironed them flat on the bed with his palms, then he slipped them into his coat pocket. He leaned down into Cecil's face and said, "You're unbelievable, Cecil!"

Stilwell said, "What?"

Folks said, "I can't understand why you don't understand, as I understand that Jimmy Dancing Rain is a fine gentleman of integrity. I'm catching the first plane to Connecticut."

Folks finished dressing and packing loose odds and ends. Cecil followed him around the room.

He said, "Alex, maybe it would be smart for me to leave, too . . . after I see Jimmy."

Folks said, "Cecil, do that so I can fly to Indiana next week to close our deal."

They heard the insistent chimes of the doorbell and Stilwell said, "I hope that's Jimmy!"

He hurried to the door and opened it to Kid. Kid stepped in and slammed shut the door behind him. He had a sad, forlorn expression on his face.

The mark said, "It's doomsday, Jimmy!"

He shoved the prop newspaper toward Kid. Kid took it and shoved it into his pocket.

Kid said, "I read it. My brother a murderer. The government has impounded Billy's millions."

The mark said, "You have my sympathy, Jimmy, but I've got big troubles, too!"

Kid put his arm around Stilwell's shoulder. He said, "Of course you have, Cecil."

Kid led the mark to a seat on the sofa. Folks followed and sat down with them.

Kid said, "The troubled must protect and comfort one another. Now, Cecil, in a calm way tell me how I can help you?"

The mark babbled, "I'm . . . a . . . respectable father and husband back home. I'm a thirty-third degree Mason. I'm the biggest, most respected citizen there is in Muncie, Indiana. I can't afford to wreck my image, my family, with notoriety or scandal! My connection with murder through our

59

deal . . . I . . . ah, well, oh Jimmy!''

Kid said, "Cecil, I can protect you. After all, I am at this moment the legal owner of record of the ghost town. I was interviewed by two treasury agents for hours. I had to come to you as immediately as I safely could to relieve your mind.''

The mark said, "Jimmy, you mean you didn't mention my name to them?''

Kid said, "Certainly not, Cecil!''

Tears brimmed in the mark's eyes. "Oh thank you so much, Jimmy. Now, about our ghost town deal . . . I . . . uh . . . .''

Kid patted his shoulder and said, "Your worries are over, Cecil.''

Kid extracted the mark's seventy-five thousand dollar instrument from his shirt pocket. He waved it, face up, before the mark's eyes to verify authenticity. Kid turned and leaned forward toward the coffee table, his back momentarily blocked the mark's field of vision. Kid palmed the real check and slipped it into his jacket breast pocket. He slipped out, from the same pocket, a replica of the mark's check. Then Kid leaned back on the sofa to unobstruct the sucker's field of vision. He tore the prop check to confetti that fell into a large ashtray. The mark flung himself across the sofa to embrace the Kid like an amorous elephant while Kid massaged the mark's shoulders.

Kid said, "Cecil, I gave my lawyer your address in Muncie and instructed him to send your confiscated fifteen thousand in cash within thirty days. He has assured me that the government can't keep it."

The mark said, "Jimmy, you're a beautiful friend!"

Kid disengaged himself. He said, "Now Cecil, our final ceremony. My deed and bill of sale."

The mark reached into his coat pocket and extracted the battered deed and bill of sale. He extended them to Kid, who took them and shredded them into the ashtray.

Folks stood up, bags in hand. He said, "Well, gentlemen, good-bye and good luck."

Folks shook hands with them.

The sucker nodded toward the ashtray and said, "My boy, I've just had good luck to remember a life time!"

Folks left to supervise a grifter crew to dismantle the ghost town and truck it into the mob's warehouse until they caught the next mark to play.

Sucker Brainstorm

4

FOLKS WENT STRAIGHT HOME after the crew had disappeared the ghost town. Pearl was delighted to see him back from the L.A. trip so soon. Folks thought, she owes her delight, of course, to the Kid's "tear up" in the "blow-off." It made it unnecessary to keep Stilwell tied up in town until his score instrument cleared.

That early evening he undelighted Pearl. Speedy and Janie were in for whist. Pearl and he were beating squawking hell out of them for the first time in a month. Then Folks' apprehension about Pappy Kid soured their fortunes. Folks played several successive hands like a novice. He wasn't, and Pearl knew it. They started yapping at each other. Janie and Speedy, of course, started having fun by skunking them soundly.

Folks thought, Pappy is booked to put Stilwell on an eight-thirty plane for the Midwest. I'm worried. He remembered the fatal propensities of Mister Stilwell and decided he had to be present. Not really present, he thought, but within reasonable proximity, until the mark is blown off on that plane.

Pearl gave him an odd look when he announced he was breaking up the card party to catch some air. To immunize his dear, precious Pearl from a tailspin into an attack of her chronic illness, he invited Speedy to tag along. On the way out, he picked up his binoculars from a table near the door.

He drove Pearl's Mercury for a change. Since I'm back to my normal blond image, the mark can't recognize me just like that, he thought. Folks knew the Kid was sticking to the mark like Elmer's Glue, and most likely keeping the mark close to the environs of his hotel until plane time. He parked in the hotel parking lot and scouted a bit. Sure enough, Kid and the mark were in the hotel coffee shop. He went back and pulled out to a parking spot across the street from the coffee shop's plate glass window. His Patek Phillippe read seven-forty-five p.m.

Within five minutes they came out to the cab stand with a bellman and Stilwell's luggage. He and Speedy followed them to the airport. Speedy stayed in the Mercury near the terminal entrance.

Folks was confident the mark couldn't recognize him. That is, he thought, unless I promenaded for him long enough to top my gait. He followed them to the second floor, at maybe a twenty-five yard range, until they reached the waiting section for upcoming departures. He went to the john adjacent to the pre-boarding section. He glanced out the window overlooking the field. The mark's plane was easing toward the embarkation tunnel on the side of the building.

He decided to risk close proximity. He took a seat in the crowded cattle pen room directly behind Stilwell. This is fun with my back almost touching the mark's, Folks thought.

The Kid gave him a dirty look for screwing around like that. Kid knew, of course, why Folks had shown up. He always pretended to be turned off by any sentimentality or protective emotional action from his bosom friends.

The clerk behind his box picked up a mike and announced, "Flight 56 now ready for boarding of passengers for Chicago, Peoria and Muncie, Indiana."

Kid and the mark stood up, shook hands and embraced. Folks was sure he should have stayed with his woman's whist to keep the peace.

The mark said, "I'll never forget you, Jimmy. I hate to say good-bye."

Kid said, "It isn't good-bye, Cecil. I'll fly out to Muncie for some of that fabulous cuisine at your restaurants that you so delightfully boast about."

The mark moved with the tide and said, "That's a wonderful idea, Jimmy. Do it soon!"

Kid said, "Soon, laddie, soon!"

Before the mark was absorbed into the crunch of departees, he turned and waved a final good-bye. Folks thought it was good-bye.

Kid said to Folks, ventriloquist style, "You lop-eared jack-off!"

Sweet old guy, the Kid, Folks thought as they went to a newsstand across the corridor for cigars and cigarettes. They made their purchases and turned away. Folks turned back to the newspaper rack to take evening papers to Pearl and Speedy, tossed the exact coins on the counter for the clerk and glanced at the headline as he joined Kid.

"*Detente Threatened*," it read.

It was the morning paper with that bold type in a square designation at the top of the front page. He said something to Kid about passe morning news as he went back for the evening paper.

The clerk noticed him rummaging the rack. He said, "Sorry sir, delivery of the evening paper is fouled up."

The clerk returned his coins. He collided with a winsome stewardess, apparently late for her flight. She tossed what looked like an airlines voucher on the counter and snatched up magazines and most of the morning papers.

The clerk turned from a customer and, as he picked up the voucher, started to shout at the stewardess. He shrugged as he decided it was useless. She had raced through the departure pen across the corridor into the door leading to the ramp.

The clerk glanced at Folks and muttered, "What the diff? Her customers can't beef about stale morning news. She's giving it away."

It hit Folks! He shoved Kid and said, "Get to Speedy in Pearl's Mercury out front! That late stewardess is taking the morning paper on flight 56."

Kid ashened and said, "I can't believe this!"

He moved out and down the corridor as Folks double-timed it down the corridor to the window of the john overlooking the field. He zeroed in on the interior of the flight 56 bird with his binoculars.

The mark was sitting relaxed in his seat. His head was thrown back on the headrest cushion. His eyes were closed. He didn't move, just opened his eyes when the stewardess reached him with her hand-outs. He smiled up at her and waved off her offer and she went down the aisle. He started to close his eyes, then he opened them and called her back. She gave him a paper and went down the aisle.

Stilwell casually flipped the newspaper open. He spread it across his lap and he stared down at it. His face transformed into maniacal rage as he leapt to his feet. His teeth flashed like fangs when he screamed. The mark was brainstorming, all right. The tumblers of the swindle had clicked into place inside his head.

He charged down the aisle in pursuit of the stewardess as the startled stewardess turned to face him. He snatched a newspaper from her and held it very close to his face as he stared at it. Then he hurled the newspaper into the aisle and snatched another newspaper. He stared at it and waggled his head furiously, then sailed the paper into the air and the aircraft started to taxi. Stilwell's teeth flashed as he hollered something.

He hurtled down the aisle past mesmerized passengers to the front exit door where a burly male flight attendant blocked his path. With the skill and violence of the ex-all American guard that he was, he linebacked the steward away to his fanny on the floor, slammed his fist down on the door lock and jumped through the opened door.

He hit the ground and tumbled before he regained his feet and charged wildly across the field toward the terminal building. He was obviously in pursuit of Pappy!

Folks bolted from the john. It took him only seconds to reach the first floor main corridor. He spotted Cecil bulling his way through alarmed people, bowling several over as he grenaded his thirteens toward the street exit. Folks reached the sidewalk seconds behind him. Speedy was just pulling from the curb.

The mark spotted Kid. He raced along side the Mercury and bellowed, "You cocksucker! You swindled me! I'll kill you!"

He leapt to the hood and smashed his fists against the windshield. Speedy turned sharply and the mark skittered off the hood onto the street. A mob of city and airport police descended on the mark.

Folks watched Speedy accelerate the Mercury out of sight, then he got a cab for Kid's place. The Kid and Speedy were cool as the snow they were snorting when he joined them. He horned in for a couple of sparkling rows.

Kid lit one of his Corona Corona's, blew a gust of powder blue smoke and said, "Laddie, the police are putting that goniff through the wringer. But he'll convince them that he has a legit complaint. I just completed a call to Captain Ellis. He's expecting you."

Kid took an envelope from a pocket of his silk lounging robe and gave it to Folks.

He said, "Get this ten percent of the score end to the captain quickly . . . before that mark can beef officially."

Folks left immediately and went to the apartment house cab stand. Fifteen minutes later, a uniformed cop showed him into Captain Ellis' office. The graying captain of bunco was sitting behind his ornate desk in the well-appointed office, sipping coffee. Folks walked to the front of his desk.

He smiled his barracuda smile. "Congratulations! Glad to see you escaped great bodily harm."

Folks said, "Thank you, Captain Ellis. But the situation never really got out of hand at the airport."

Folks reached into his coat pocket to extract the pay-off envelope. He leaned toward the captain and placed it on the desk top. The captain ignored the envelope.

Folks said, "There's Kid's full premium . . . ten percent of ninety thousand dollars . . . for the Stilwell coverage."

The captain took a sip of coffee and dabbed a linen handkerchief against his heavy lips before he said, "I don't know about that. Perhaps I shouldn't issue a policy on Stilwell for ten percent."

Folks said, "Captain, if you up your share, it's gonna bruise the score."

He smiled. "Bruise the score, or kick it back to Stilwell! I want fifteen percent!"

Folks said, "But Captain, I'm not qualified to make a decision like that."

He leaned back and said, "Wonder, you're much too modest. You're qualified to know that a con store is like a house of wax. It can't survive strong heat without a strong fix!"

Folks said, "But Captain, Mr. Stilwell has blown off his heavy steam."

The captain leaned his massive frame toward Folks with his eyes flickering green flame. He half whispered, "Don't play the con for me, Wonder. I knew what happened at the airport five minutes after it blew. Even the Vicksburg Kid couldn't blow that mark off. That mark is hot enough to fry this administration! Face it! I could demand fifty percent of the score and deserve it. I'm the only one qualified now who can blow him off."

Folks said, "Well Captain, I don't have your five percent puff up. Sure, you're worth it, Captain Ellis, but I'll have to expose the Kid to your logic."

The phone rang. Captain Ellis picked up and said, "Yes . . . yes . . . ."

He stared up at Folks as he listened. He said, "Yes, Officer Tate! Go on . . . ."

He leaned back in his chair, reached into his baroque humidor and extracted an imported Panatella. He said, "Wonder, light my cigar."

Folks smiled as he went around the desk and flicked his lighter flame to Ellis' cigar tip as he listened on the phone with a "rapist laid the virgin" look.

Folks said, "Captain, we're lucky to have a stand-up friend like you."

He frowned him silent. Ellis said, "All right! Give me ten minutes, Officer Tate, before you bring Stilwell in."

He hung up and said, "Mr. Stilwell has indicated a determination to beef past me, should I fail to satisfy his lust for justice. This is bad! I can only see a kickback of the score to Stilwell, or indictments, unless I blow-off that mark. I want twenty percent of the score."

Folks said, "Captain, you're great! Just priceless! So, you got your twenty percent! Captain, no disrespect, but may I be excused before you wind up with the long end of the score?"

The captain blew a mote of cigar ash off the sleeve of his five "C" note suit. His five carat ring shot light like a swarm of fireflies. He chuckled, "You're a charmer, Utah Wonder. I like you."

Folks said, "I'm fond of you too, Captain. Any chance I get the exclusive right to light all of your cigars?"

He said evenly, "I'll expect you here before noon tomorrow."

Folks nodded and smiled as he left the office for the street. He stood in the neon thicket looking for a cab, whistled at one that was in hire. A pastel fox, in a pink Excalibur, flushed from the thicket. Christina Buckmeister pulled to the curb in front of him. She waggled a long, tapered finger his way.

She swung the Excalibur door open, his side. Her

eyes were slumberous, beclouded with vulva steam and he got in. She threw her head back and laughed with joy. He saw her nostrils were frosted with crystal blow dust. She sucked his bottom lip.

He thought, what the hell. Why not punish this come freak with my ten inch whip?

Behind them, on the sidewalk, one of Captain Ellis' bunco detectives stared at them with a surprised and thoughtful look on his corrugated face. He went into Captain Ellis' office, reported the scene he'd witnessed and left the office.

Captain Ellis went through a familiar routine. He swiveled his chair to remove a folder fat with Canadian dossiers and mug shots from a filecase behind his desk bearing the caption *Vicksburg Kid And Associates*. Captain Ellis put it into his desk drawer and locked it. He turned back to the filecase and extracted folders and mug shots of deceased and imprisoned con men. He placed them on the desk before him.

Officer Tate escorted Stilwell into the office. The captain slipped on his commiserating blow-off-the-mark mask as Officer Tate deposited Stilwell into a chair at the side of the desk. The captain smiled and leaned to give Stilwell's hand an energetic shake reserved for transient V.I.P.'s and city hall nabobs. The captain lit a cigar as Stilwell started his fruitless search of the mug shots.

5

CHRISTINA LIT a stick of gangster for them. Folks studied her perfect profile, her breeze-flogged hair streamed like golden bunting as she hustled the Excalibur through the moil of cars and people to the outskirts of the city. He marveled at her sorcerous resemblance, under the soft glow of the night sky, to Camille Costain, the alabaster Chicago witch with the kinky sexual hang-ups with rain and the psychic maim as keys to the penultimate sexual gratification. He remembered again how Camille had tortured him, driven him to near madness before she dumped him.

Christina said, "How about a bit of this lovely night's ambience before I drop you off, wherever?"

Folks shrugged, "Why not?"

She smiled, inserted Robert Goulet's "Couldn't We?" into a dashboard tape deck and sang along throatily.

Folks decided to postpone Christina's direct physical punishment through a brutal womb sweep with his weapon. He'd titillate her, ignite a bonfire of passion in her loins, get his revenge on her for the Costain pain. He'd leave her strung up on a steamy rack of desire and frustration. He'd punish Christina, the heiress, for the crimes of her robber baron fore-bearers, for her death-stained fortune. The fortune amassed from the misery of coal mine's black lungers, he'd read so much about to support his fake background as Utah Wonder, star con roper up from the coal pits.

He'd punish her for the hopelessness and starvation in black ghettos, for his dead black mother. For all the blacks ever imprisoned in holds of slave-ships. He'd punish her for being spoiled, pampered, aggressive, beautiful and rich. But most of all for the pain her prototype, Camille Costain, had inflicted upon him. He shaped a cruel smile as she tooled the Excalibur into an access road at the foot of a mountain.

Suddenly she pulled the car onto the road shoulder. She dramatically keyed off the engine, turned and faced him with an enigmatic smile.

He suspected she was about to give him some sort of crotch test to reverse their positions. He blandly looked about the moon-swept, but rather bleak terrain in the loom of the stygian mountain.

He mockingly said, "Miss Buckmeister, this is an

interesting spot that you've discovered. A macabre ambience."

She glanced toward the mountain and said huskily, "Johnny, I didn't want to stop here. I did because I'm afraid of you, Johnny." She fingered the lacy hem of her slip as she averted her eyes. "I wanted us to go to my lodge at the top of the mountain, but you . . . ah, well, lie for a living. I hate lies! I've never before felt for any man quite as I do about you. I'm terrified at the risk that you, the consummate reflex liar, have lost the capacity for truth in every instance. I pressured Trevor to tell me all about you, how you, a child of fourteen, went into the Utah mines to support your mother and younger brothers and sisters. That is your redeeming aspect to me. Otherwise I should not be here with you. The question is whether your horrid life left you bitter and hostile toward people like me."

He slipped on a wounded mask and stared ahead. "There is no reason to fear me. But I don't plan to take a polygraph test to convince you of that, Miss Buckmeister."

She was unsmiling, phosphorescent in her diaphanous white silk dress. She gazed at his sculpted Errol Flynn profile. She was motionless, like a pastel mannequin in the star-lit window of night.

He decided that he could better frustrate her, maim her, get the hook sunk deeply into her psyche up there in her web. He thought, this assassin needs to con me that she's afraid like Camille did before she slaughtered me. He shaped his heartbreaking

74

little boy smile and took her into his arms. They deep-tongued.

He disengaged and whispered, "Christina, please don't be afraid. I could never lie to you, darling. You can risk the mountain top."

He tried vainly to remember the novelist who had propounded the theory that all black men had been driven insane in the throes of the fake great nightmare, American Dream. Was he insane?

She put the car in motion and catapulted the sleek machine up the mountain through caverns of lush spicy forests to its top. She parked before the stately redwood lodge, gleaming richly on the moon-engorged pinnacle. The shimmering neon below was strung about the city's frame like ropes of rainbow pearls.

She slid from the car, stood like a quizzical Botticelli nymph, to see him look blandly at her, make no effort to follow her lead. She laughed, "Johnny, I can't believe that you want *me* to carry you past the threshold."

He smiled, "Come back here to me, darling. Let's enjoy the view a bit."

With transient pout, she got in, wiggled herself snugly against him, her cheek against his chest. She goosebumped him with her nails across the blue silk at his kneecap. His fingertip caressed the passion pit beneath her earlobe to stoke her crotch fire as they gazed down at the extravaganza of city lights.

He thought about the walk-up tenement hovels and the zillion meals missed in the Chicago black ghetto. The senseless cuttings and shootings behind

75

the psychotic invisible walls of the ghetto. He remembered how the icy winds had slashed him blue with cold through his threadbare garments going to school and his lunches of fatback and turnip greens sandwiches.

He remembered the arrest of the gaunt old man on a street corner, his black face deformed before his pauper audience with revolutionary passion as he shouted, "The rich should be compelled, at gun point, to share their riches with the starving wretched masses. We blacks must force all white offspring of their slavemaster fathers to pay us reparations for the sweat and agony of our slave mothers and fathers."

Reparations! The concept burst like a thunderbolt inside his head. He was electrified at the realization that he held the palpitating heiress to the Buckmeister millions in his arms. He thought, I must play her for the ultimate stakes. Of course, he told himself, my real, noble purpose must be to lock up this gold-plated bitch. Marry her! Then find the method to use the most of her fortune for reparations, the rest for my personal future and security, before I dump her.

He trembled with excitement at the birth of his master plan for her. He thought about Pearl and the certain complications. He'd structure that aspect later, he decided. In the blinding brilliance of his master plan he wondered if Pearl was indeed indispensable. He thought, I must first discover what Christina is to the bone.

Christina said, "Are you chilled? I felt you

76

shiver, Johnny."

He said, "No, I'm comfortable."

He remembered the Vicksburg Kid had told him about how Christina's late grifter father had built the foundation for the Buckmeister empire in Germany from stock and bond flim flams. And before that the hoary money machine swindle. He'd sound her out, play her, convince her and fleece her as he would any other mark. Poetic justice for the daughter of a con man.

He said, "Tell me about your aristocratic self."

She chewed her bottom lip. "Johnny, until Victoria, my mother, became ill, my life in my memory has always been a cliche poor little rich girl existence, dangling on a dominating, possessive maternal string. With Victoria's guidance I accepted the challenge of managing the family's business affairs. My new responsibilities have given me at least the chance to escape vegetation and the means to hold at bay the drooling cabal of alleged men who hounded me around the clock. But now I'm suffering from emotional dehydration. Johnny, I need a man I want. I want to be happy, to be fulfilled. I'm an executive by necessity. But, I'm first a woman. Oh Johnny, I'm so lonely!"

He said, "I'm lonely, too."

She said, "Is that why you and that black woman had dinner together the other night?"

He said, "Not exactly. She's just a friend. I'm able to advise her on certain business problems thanks to a degree in business administration. I know her family."

Christina sighed, "I'm relieved to hear that, Johnny."

He said, "Why?"

She said, "Because Latins and blacks are notorious for low boiling points, especially when their romantic links are snarled by white women. I'm strongly attracted to you Johnny, but I wouldn't be thrilled at the prospect of mayhem or worse as a result of whatever territoriality I might enjoy with you. To say nothing of the scandal! Johnny, do you have any serious affair going?"

He decided to swing the gate wide. "Why, no. I like it that way. Please don't plan to get me into trouble."

She laughed, "You can't be unaware that I already have."

They lit cigarettes.

She said, "Where do you live, Johnny?"

He said, "On the west side. I share an apartment with Speedy, your chief of security, and his girl."

She said, "When should I call you to catch you in an emergency? Such as I just have to hear the sound of your voice."

He knew that Speedy's girl, Janie, was in L.A. for a couple of weeks. And Speedy seldom left for the Buckmeister place until four p.m. He said, "Before four on weekdays."

She said, "Fine, I have the number." She stroked her fingertips across his inner thigh, "Let's go inside. I'll buy you a drink."

His cue, he thought, to "prat" her out, block her away from the erotic payoff in the sure shot tradition of the con. The cinch way to hype up her passion and desire for him, to lower the odds in his favor for his total conquest of her.

He glanced at his watch, kissed her and said, "I'm afraid I'm very late for that business appointment I was on my way to keep when you picked me up. Darling, I'm so sorry we can't explore our . . . uh, intimate possibilities in the unhurried way I think we should. Let's make a date to meet on this spot."

She moved beneath the wheel, started the car and said peevishly, "All right, Johnny. When?"

He enjoyed an interior smirk as he thought about the way Camille Costain had "pratted" him out to wildly palpitate him with the yen to sex her. "Johnny, let me miss you until I'm bursting inside," she purred. "Let's wait until we can make love to the music of a rainstorm."

Folks said, "Christina, let's rush here to meet the very next time it rains, at its first fall. Think of the sweet mystique of it, darling, lying in soft shadows wrapped in the heady drama of a rainstorm, even salutes of thunder, with a light show of lightning."

She kissed him hungrily and exclaimed, "It's a dynamite idea, Johnny!" She turned the car around and as she drove down the road, she said, "I'll miss you . . . where should I drop you?"

He answered, "The Marriott."

They were practically silent all the way downtown. He kissed her, got out in front of the hotel, paused at the driver's side.

She said, "Goodnight Johnny. I hope it you know what's soon, otherwise I'll have to hire a squadron of aircraft to seed the clouds!"

He smiled. "Goodnight, Angel Face. Between us we'll pull down a lulu of a rainstorm soon!"

He went into the hotel lobby and watched her gun the Excalibur away into the neon thickets. He purchased a dozen red roses from the hotel's florist. Then he went to the street and got into a cab for home. And Pearl.

Pearl was in the bathroom when he walked into his apartment. He got into lounging clothes and propped himself in bed to read the newspaper. It struck him that Pearl's rich contralto voice was not accompanying the lyrics of running water as she washed stockings and underthings as usual. A moment later, he looked up from the paper and smiled when she opened the door and stepped into the bedroom in her panties.

He held out his arms and said, "Hi, sweetheart. How about some hot bubbling sugar?"

Pearl came to the bed with something concealed in her hand. She bypassed his upturned lips and pecked him on the forehead.

He said, "You got a cold, baby?"

She shook her head and sat on the side of the bed facing him. Her glaring brown eyes in the smear of cold cream on her tar black face gave the effect of an angry Mau Mau maiden. She retreated her wrist as he reached to touch it.

He said, "Tough day at school today, huh?"

She said, "No, tough time when I found your

stash of dope on the floor beneath the facebowl in the bathroom." She opened her hand and thrust a small cellophane package on her palm into his face.

He stared at it, realized that the Scotch tape had given way and exposed his passion for cocaine. He said, "Hon, don't be uptight. That isn't dope. I mean, it isn't H. A joker laid it on me to try. It's coke, sugar face . . . a harmless recreational high."

He reached to take the quarter ounce of precious dust. She ripped open the package and dumped the powder into a pitcher of water on a nightstand beside the bed. He groaned, "Oh, you square-ass broad! You just blew several 'C' notes!"

She said, "Ah ha! You lied! Junkie, you bought that dope! I'm not so square that I don't know dope that expensive isn't passed out as freebie samples. Who are you really, Johnny? What are you? I want to know! Now!"

He said, "I'm Johnny O'Brien, real estate speculator. I'm willing to forget your vandalism with that coke if you can get yourself together and forget."

She said, with heat, "I can't accept that, and the rest of the mysterious shit about you. I mean it, Johnny! I can't live like this. I must have answers to questions that have made me miserable since I left Canada with you."

Folks' blue eyes were radiant with aggravation. He said, "All right, sweet stuff, take an enema. Fire away!"

She said, "For an opener, what do you and Saul Borenstein really do for a living?"

He looked at her, a portrait of doubt and suspicion with her legs crossed, elbow propped on her thigh with her chin resting in her palm, glaring at him. For the hundredth time since he'd known her he flirted with telling her the truth. It was her fault that forced my lies, he told himself. Rather, her strait-laced black middle class brainwashed dogma about honesty and hard, legitimate labor as the only acceptable means to realize the so-called American Dream.

Impatient to skewer him, she said, "C'mon, Slick Johnny, tell it like it is. Try the truth on me for a change. I care enough to try to accept even dope dealing."

He shaped a bitter little smile. It had been her naivete, her honesty, fidelity and rare purity of heart that had attracted him, made him want her for his woman. Now it was too late for the truth, he told himself. She'll freak out with paranoia and hatred for a gee in her bed who lies for a living. My ego trapped me. Jesus Christ! I was insecure. I wanted her because she adored me, wasn't a threat like most women who play men in the pit against other men and pussy power games. He was sorry she was hurting. But what could he do?

He decided to give her as much truth as he dared. Christina and his reparations master plan flashed through his head. How could he ever share that with Pearl? He felt his first grave doubt as to whether they would be able to go on together much longer.

He reached to stroke her hair but she recoiled. He sighed, "Baby, Saul and I sell real estate. That's the guaranteed truth. We . . . uh, well, unethically resell the same property again and again. But, sweetheart, the saving grace is that we only . . . uh, well, cheat only greedy white buyers, thieves at heart who are out to cheat us—crooks, I swear, who are wealthy and can afford to be cheated, that need to be taught a lesson. I promise to get out of the business, maybe within a year. We'll have enough money then to open that fabulous day care center for pre-schoolers that you dream about. Trust me, baby!"

He stared at her flabbergasted as she burst into tears, tumbled to the carpet and rolled herself into an agonized fetal ball. Shaken, he leapt from the bed to her side on his haunches. He tried to take her into his arms.

She gouged a red line with fingernails across his hand and blubbered savagely. "Don't touch me! I'll tear out your eyes! Liar!"

He sat on the side of the bed and watched her roll pitifully in her tantrum. His face was deformed with aggravation and angry frustration. He said, "Pearl, I told you the truth, as much as you're going to get for now. Now pull yourself together and act like a woman!"

She clapped her palms over her ears and babbled in her misery. "You bastard! You lied! I know about title insurance and real estate abstracts. The police would bury you and Saul in prison and lose the key the first time you tried a deal. Wealthy people aren't that stupid. Be fair, Johnny. Why hurt me? You said you wanted me with you always in Canada. I was doing all right until you came along with your lies. I had a man, a kind man who loved me, trusted me. I broke his heart for you. Oh, God! Don't I deserve the simple truth for that, Johnny? Liar! Liar!" She rolled and sobbed piteously on the carpet.

He decided he couldn't take any more. He couldn't run down how the cunning structure of the long con made the real estate swindle work. He regretted that he had told her anything. So, he eased away to spend the night across the hall with Speedy.

She finally got to her feet and went toward the bathroom to wash her face. She stopped, did a double take at his blue silk suit jacket draped across a chair in a lance of bathroom light. She plucked a glittery Christina Buckmeister strand of golden hair from the jacket, studied it, held it to the light between her fingertips. Then she flung it away as if it were a cobra. She cried out like a scalded infant and renewed her wild weeping.

At that moment, at the airport, Captain Ellis and Stilwell stood in a crowd of passengers waiting at an embarkation entrance to a mid-west flight. A con mob tailer stood behind them eavesdropping. The captain and Stilwell locked hands in a warm handshake.

Stilwell said, "Thank you again, Captain Ellis, for your sympathy and counsel. I was in a bad way about all that money."

The captain embraced his shoulders. "Mister Stilwell, it has been an extraordinary pleasure to meet you and serve you. I vow to catch those crooked dogs that bit you!"

Stilwell said, "Captain, you keep your promise and I'll keep mine to fly back to witness against them."

The captain rippled his jaw muscles. "Cecil, in the name of the Lord, I'll keep my vow!"

They embraced. Stilwell turned and went into the embarkation tunnel with the crowd. Kid's tailer hurried to a phone to give Kid the good blow-off news.

6

THE VICKSBURG KID called Folks and Speedy the next morning, Saturday, to a meeting. Folks drove his Eldorado. Rita let Folks and Speedy into the Kid's posh high-rise apartment, led them into the den, then returned to a stool and her glass at the redwood bar. Aristocratic looking High Pockets Kate and High Ass Marvel, the full-blooded Indian, bloody-eyed with a hangover, were in chairs grouped in a close semi-circle around the wire thin, silver-thatched Kid seated on the sofa.

Kid said, "Sit down here on the sofa, laddies."

They sat down, flanking Kid.

Kid glanced at his wristwatch. "Trevor is late as usual, so I won't delay the fabulous good news." Kid paused to light a Pantella. "On a scale of ten, friends, I've gotten a line on a ten-plus mark. He's sweet! *Nouveau riche* ex-cowboy, rodeo slob. Married a kooky sucker fan of the manure-and-bruises circuit. Her millions have made Marvin Bates, the bum, a cattle ranch baron. I received the research report on them just this morning. Bates satisfies all the criteria for the perfect mark played against The Unhappy Virgin. His personality priority is greed. He's a cutthroat savage with a hard-on for "The Best Of It." In addition, he's an immoral buffoon with a wild eye for fancy fluffs. Rita is making her debut with us as the requisite sex-pot distraction for Bates. He has a commercial hang-up for sunken, ancient ships which the treasure lure of the Virgin presents irresistibly."

Kid picked up an edition of the *Wall Street Journal* from the coffee table, slapped it against his palm. "A *Journal* article reports that Bates, for months, has had difficulty getting his price for sale of a ranch outside the city. He has taken up temporary residence in a downtown hotel suite. He has also set up an office in town. He's there six days a week."

Kid beamed a knowing smile at Folks as he gave Folks the *Journal.*

Folks took the cue. He said, "Kid, I love it! I cut into Bates as a buyer for the ranch, then rope him for the play. Kid, what kind of score do you see?"

Kid said, "Wonder, with Bates' level of liquid capital and the quality play we can give him now with our mansion-museum set-up, so beautifully ready, I see a mil score . . . if, of course, you hook and reel in Bates in your usual air tight fashion.''

Kid stood to signal the end of the meeting. He eye signaled Folks and Speedy to remain as he followed the mob to the front door. Kid shut the door and led Folks and Speedy back to the den sofa, then frowned as he leaned toward a tape recorder on the coffee table.

He said, "Laddies, this is a bit of taped conversation from Speedy's bug in Victoria Buckmeister's bedroom between herself and Trevor." Kid turned on the machine.

Victoria spoke. *"Why, oh why, Trevor, did you not attend the affair given by the MacDills for Catherine?"*

Trevor said, *"Mother, you're very ill and I don't really want to argue with you again about your compulsion to play Cupid. I refuse to romance that utter bore, Catherine MacDill."*

Victoria said, *"You prefer the trollops and tramps in the gutter . . . your father was like that! Trevor, you'll debauch yourself out of the possibility of an advantaged marriage with a peer. I no longer have the expectation that you can become the ideal Buckmeister man."*

The sound of Trevor's fingers snapping was heard as he replied, *"Mother, I know how to please you!"*

Victoria said, *"Yes, Trevor."*

With heavy sarcasm, Trevor said, *"I'll marry Chris. That way no outsider can take pot shots at Buckmeister money. That is your major concern, isn't it, Mother?"*

88

Victoria's voice shook with anger. "*I'll cane you!*"

There was the sound of it cracking against a hard surface and a scrambling noise.

Apparently the invalid Victoria said from her bed, "*Come here, Trevor!*"

Trevor said, "*I will not let you brain me. You've forgotten, Mother, whom you must depend on as head of our business interests.*"

Victoria said, "*Did depend on, Trevor. As of this moment, I am putting Christina in charge.*"

Victoria, the heart patient, was heard gasping for air.

"*You worthless gutter snipe! You've given me an attack! Millie! Millie!*" Victoria choked out.

The sounds of the nurse's voice and urgent footsteps were heard.

Then Trevor's voice. "*Mother, I'm sorry, deeply sorry you've forced me to upset you again.*"

Kid cut off the machine. He said. "I hope the old lady cools off and forgets that crack about kicking Trevor off the top spot. Our fix for our set-up could curdle fast with his sister calling the shots at the bank. And Trevor's clout with the police brass downtown could fizzle if he's demoted. What a lousy fall of cards with Bates, the perfect mark, on the turn."

Folks said, "Should I cut into Bates and rope him anyway?"

Kid sighed, "Why the hell not? This afternoon is not too soon. We've got to play for that mil! Maybe I can give Trevor an angle or two to ease him into

Victoria's good graces. Officially he's still in charge."

Folks said, "Kid, I can't say that it's worth much at this point, but Christina appears to have the hots for me."

Kid said, "It could be an angle to keep our operation fixed." He shrugged elaborately, "But with a nitro fluff like that, there's no bedrock stability. Be careful. Don't shake her up! She could blow us into the pen!"

Folks and Speedy left the apartment to pick up a rented limo. They waved at Trevor, in his white Continental, driving toward the Kid's apartment house. After renting the limo, they drove to their apartment building, while Folks and Speedy went into Speedy's apartment across the hall from Folks' own. Speedy costumed himself in dove gray chauffeur's attire.

Folks called Bates' office to make an afternoon appointment, then prepared himself for the Bates cut-in before Speedy's dresser mirror. He covered his blond hair with an undetectable curly black wig and a fake thick moustache, both with the sheen of a raven's breast. He inserted brown contact lenses over his blue eyes. Then he costumed himself elegantly in a midnight blue Brooks Brother's suit, gray hombrug hat, handmade black wing tip shoes, blue silk tie and snowy linen. Then he slipped on platinum-rimmed spectacles.

He was pleased as he studied himself in the mirror, confident that he looked the part of Lance Wellington, scion of a vast English fortune. He walked into the living room.

Speedy, seated on a couch, stared at him, whistled as he made an A-OK circle with his fingers. He said, "Folks, you're perfect!"

Folks replied in a cultured, crisp British accent. "Thank you very much, my dear man. Shall we go to cut . . . uh, rather, I mean, to keep my appointment with Mister Bates?"

They laughed and went to the limo. Speedy drove it downtown, pulling it into Bates' building parking lot. Folks went to the building elevators and got into one, stepped out on the fifth floor. He walked down a corridor to an office door stenciled *Lone Star Incorporated.* In lower case beneath that, *Marvin L. Bates and Associates.* Folks opened the door and stepped into a plush reception room.

He said, "Good afternoon. I'm Lance Wellington."

A handsome, mature woman was behind a desk. A pair of big-eyed pre-teen twin girls, with a marked resemblance to the woman, stared at him from a leather couch.

The woman smiled and said, "Good afternoon, Mister Wellington. I'm Mrs. Bates." She picked up an intercom phone and said, "Marvin, Mister Wellington is here." She nodded toward a door across the room.

Folks said, "Thank you, Mrs. Bates." He went across the carpet to the door, opened it and stepped into the large room.

Giant Bates rose to his feet behind his massive mahogany desk. He leaned across it with a huge paw extended and a broad smile on his bald-pated, seamed face. "Howdy do, Mister Wellington!"

91

he exclaimed, in a heavy Texas accent, as Folks shook his hand.

"Very well, thank you, Mister Bates," Folks said as he placed his business card on the desk top. He sat down in a chair facing the desk.

Bates picked up the card and studied it for a moment. Bates said, "European ski resorts, interesting Mr. Wel . . . aw heck, can't we drop our last names, Lance?"

Folks smiled, "Why not, Marvin?" He fluttered the *Wall Street Journal* in his hand as he leaned toward Bates. "Marvin, I have plans to diversify my investments. I envision the largest dude ranch in the world here in the States. The description, the location of your property that you wish to sell, seems to fit my requirements. Marvin, I should like to tour it at your convenience."

Bates said, "I would enjoy showing it to you, Lance, at your covenience. As you know it's just over the state line in Nevada, a short, pleasant hour ride from here."

Folks said, "Splendid, Marvin. I'll call you early next week and arrange the trip."

Bates said, "That will be just great, Lance."

They stood and shook hands.

Mrs. Bates entered the room. She placed a sheaf of papers on the desk.

Bates said, "Georgia, this gentleman wants to be the head honcho of the largest dude ranch in the world."

She looked at Folks wide-eyed.

Folks said, "I confess to that ambition, Mrs.

92

Bates."

She said, "I grew up on one, even managed one in later years. Do you have experience in the field?"

Folks said, "No, I don't. I'll need a competent manager."

She said, "Management of such an enterprise has its peculiar problems. Should you acquire our property, I would be delighted to put you in touch with the proper people."

Bates said, "Now, Georgia, let's not give Mr. Wellington the idea that we are in some kind of hard sell cahoots."

Mrs. Bates blushed in apparent embarrassment. She moved from behind the desk and went toward the door.

She said, "Mister Wellington, I hope I did not give you that impression."

Folks said, "Certainly not, Mrs. Bates."

She said, "Thank you, Mister Wellington!" She turned to Bates. "You see, Marvin, Mister Wellington didn't misunderstand me in the least." She triumphantly left the room.

Folks and Bates moved to the door and Bates opened it.

Bates said, "Lance, I always thought the British were stuffed shirts until I met you. In just an hour I enjoy your company like I would a close home boy."

Folks smiled, "Thank you, Marvin. My maternal great grandmother was a homegirl from Dallas. That alone seals our friendship."

They laughed.

Bates winked salaciously. He said, "Lance, my boy, you gotta be some kind of poontanger with the girls." Bates darted a wary eye toward Mrs. Bates at her desk. Bates whispered, "Maybe we can drive into Vegas for a hot minute and lasso some he-man fun."

Folks returned his wink. "I'm certain that we will find something, Marvin." Folks, imitating Bates, darted a furtive eye toward Mrs. Bates. He lowered his voice. "Something well-rounded and orgasmic in Silicone Gulch."

They laughed. Folks turned to leave and Bates banged a ham-hock hand against Folks' shoulder.

Bates said, "Lance, my boy, you're my kind of gentleman!"

They warmly shook hands. Folks left the office and went to the elevator athrob with satisfaction that the Bates cut-in had come off so sweetly.

Bates, shark undercover Treasury Department agent, went to his phone to call his immediate superior with the news that the Vicksburg Kid's con mob had gobbled their meticulously prepared bait and that the government's investigation of Federal Bank Act violations by the Buckmeister Bank was proceeding as planned.

Hate Bangs a Dream

7

NEXT DAY, beneath a cloudy Sunday sky, the mob had set up the ghost town in a remote, hidden ravine ten miles from the city. They had earlier performed a dress rehearsal for the upcoming Bates play at the mansion-museum set-up. Now they were concluding rehearsals with Folks in the key role of Aztec Billy. Speedy filled in as Bates, the mark.

One of the trooper grifters from the Stilwell play was closely observing Folks' performance as Billy to prep himself to play it for Bates. The other fake trooper from the Stilwell play had taken Folks' Lance Wellington role.

The Kid, earlier that morning, had bailed out High Ass Marvel from jail. The charges were disorderly conduct and aggravated assault on police officers stemming from a drunken brawl late Saturday night in a fashionable downtown bar. Something to do with Marvel's unrequited heat for a barfly sexpot and her ex-pug bird dog.

Kid had berated Marvel with master works of profanity for his drinking and cavalier attitude toward the Kid's iron-clad rule that his players keep a low public profile. High Ass, in Apache pique, had caught the first thing smoking out of the city.

At twilight the mob completed the final bidding segment of the rehearsal in the stable. One of the troopers would stay as a watchman until the Bates play.

There was a flash of lightning and rain fell heavily. Folks thought of his promised rendezvous with Christina at her mountain lodge. He grinned as he decided to keep the date costumed as ragamuffin Aztec Billy. He thought, I'll shock and tantalize the jaded witch!

Folks and Speedy got in Trevor's Continental, and the others got into their cars and went down the ghost town's muddy street for the highway.

Pearl pulled her Mercury from the cover of a stand of trees on a rise overlooking the ghost town. She drove down the hill and continued her all-day tailing as Folks drove his Eldorado down the highway through thick curtains of rain to keep his tryst with Christina.

Pearl was caught at a stoplight near the obscure dirt turn-off road leading to Christina's lodge. She drove frantically up and down the highway, her eyes vainly searched motel and restaurant parking

lots on both sides of the highway for Folks' Eldorado. Finally, she parked in a McDonald's lot at
the intersection where she had lost him. She sipped
coffee in her car with a tight face as she grimly
hawkeyed the rain-fogged highway traffic moving
in both directions through bellowing thunder and
dazzling spears of lightning.

Folks and Christina sat cozily in the luxurious
lodge on a couch before a warming, incandescent
log in the fireplace that grenaded sparks. They
snorted sparkling rows of cocaine with a mother-
of-pearl horn. In the vermillion flare of the flames
Christina's curves gleamed through a black organza
peignoir. Robert Goulet's "Couldn't We?" pulsed
softly from a console.

Christina's eyes were oddly electric, sweeping
Folks' battered boots, his tattered combination ancient Indian and southwest cowboy garb as he
leaned snorting cocaine off the coffee table. A fake
Cortez era helmet was jammed down over his
shoulder-length platinum wig to his ears. His red-
tinted face was creased and ruined with artificial
age. His front teeth were blacked out with tar.

Rain stomped a raucous flamenco on the slate
roof as she leaned and nibbled at his earlobe. She
whispered, "Aztec Billy, you're adorable!"

He sat back. She sucked his nipple through a
hole in his shirt. Then, she swooped her head and
teethed his fly open, gnawing at his pubic hair.
In return he daggered a fingernail down her spine
making her shiver and squeal.

In the earthy dialect of Billy, he said, "You boil

my pot and I'm gonna give your poontang a black eye!"

They laughed and she snorted up a row of crystal dust. Folks got a quality erection as he brutally pinched her buttocks and gazed at her classic profile, translucent in kleigs of lightning. She trembled as she gazed luminous, enormous eyes into his. His slab of weapon escaped his fly into the firelight.

She caressed it and whispered, "Billy, your womb duster is heroic. And how your eyes turn me on. Up! Up! High! To randy heaven. Your eyes are like swatches of Saint Tropez sky in summer. Gorgeous Johnny and fantasy. One!"

He tried to remember that broad who had said something like that before about his eyes but couldn't.

She purred on, "I'd love to share a secret with you, Billy. You're a living link up with fantasy and dreams I've had since a little girl. There is this grotesque, but utterly exciting old roue. Shrinks tell me he was the symbol of my repressed desire to copulate with Father. Billy, you don't think I'm a freak?"

He shook his head.

She said, "Then make love to me like that cruel old roue. Maim me with your dong! Ball me until I beg you for mercy. But don't give me any." She giggled. "Will you promise to keep it a secret from Johnny?"

He said, "I will if you will."

They laughed. She slipped out of her wrapper, then removed his boots. He, wearing the wig and helmet, stripped nude. His blood-bloated organ lobbed a fearsome shadow across her flame-tinted torso as he lifted her into his arms. He arranged her bottom meat, with the casual precision of a butcher, on a pillow placed on a crotch high table block with her back jammed against the wall.

He shaped a cruel smile as he watched his reflection in a wall mirror trap her legs across the ridges of his shoulders. Then he lacerated her swollen Bing cherry nipples, lips and tongue with his bared teeth. She squawked ecstatically as she bucked in the trap. He gripped his weapon and twirled the snout violently against her clit until her vulva frothed with lubricity. Tidal waves of rapture rocked him to perversely imagine himself, like Hitler's Rommel, juggernaut into the enemy, blitz her thicketed enclave pit with tank-like, powerful reams of his steely armament.

She trembled the air with howls of joy and pain. Dispassionately, he counted ten orgasmic spasms of her entrails as his weapon concussed her pit with a tally of five hundred bludgeon strokes. She sighed and went ragdoll limp. He stared down at her corrupt child's face in repose, sweat shiny in the flickering firelight.

His unconquered slab of vengeance made a kissy sound withdrawing. He had no need or desire for anti-climactic physical ejaculation. He had achieved climax, an orgasm in his soul. He carried her to the couch, then went to the bathroom and brought an icy towel for her face. She stirred and opened her eyes, smiled and seized him in her arms, pulling him down between her thighs. They gazed into each others eyes.

She said, "Aztec Billy, I love you."

He frowned skepticism. "Darling, don't lead my poor heart to slaughter. Don't you mean you love our loving?"

Hurt ridged her brows for an instant. Her golden mane swirled about her shoulders as she shook her head vigorously. "Please believe me. I mean I'm certain I loved you from the instant I saw you."

"Aztec Billy loves you, darling!" He stripped off the Cortez helmet and wig. "Christina, Johnny O'Brien loves you too." He shaped his heartbreaking smile. "Is it possible that you can love both of us? Billy and me?"

She laughed. "I love you both equally and madly."

He slipped off, from his pinky, the heirloom Unhappy Virgin ring. Taking her hand, he said, "Could it be a mistake to dream the sweetest dream I could ever dream?"

She raised her ring finger with an outcry of joy as he slid on the ring. They kissed torridly.

She said, "I'm so happy I want to shout from steeples! I've landed in a bed of orchids with the man I love."

He was intoxicated as heady victory shot thrilly lances through his being. Then he sobered, remembering his Pearl problem adangle. He simply needed time, he thought, to angle a solution.

He said, "Please, angel face, don't shout it until after Saul and I have concluded a business deal with a mar . . . uh, client. A Mister Bates this month. The announcement of our engagement would magnetize local newspaper reporters and photographers. I am associated with Bates as Lance Wellington, and we could save him confusion by keeping our secret until after he's gone home to the east coast. Do you understand, darling?"

"Of course you're right. I couldn't stand a misadventure now." Then she frowned. "Johnny, promise me that you'll retire from the rotten confidence game after we marry."

"I promise."

They lay in the fire-lit shadows for a long while before they showered and dressed. They clung together for a final kiss before they went to their cars, a perfect meld of sadist and masochist in the pungent murk.

Folks drove down the stygian mountain darkness toward the highway followed by Christina's Excalibur. He glanced through the windshield at the obese full moon as it suddenly smashed through a wall of clouds. He thought, you wonderful, mystical old broad, you're in the family way with a billion golden dreams. Then he thought about Pearl prophetically. And maybe nightmares.

Pearl, in the fallen dark on the McDonald's parking lot, saw Folks go past her in the Eldorado. She keyed on the Mercury's motor, started to back out to go down the driveway to the highway to follow. Then she stiffened to see Christina pull to a stop at the red light scant yards from her at the intersection. She hurtled the Mercury over the sidewalk onto the highway broadside across the front of the Excalibur. Curious motorists gaped as she leapt from the Mercury and sprinted to the driver's side of Christina's car. Pearl jerked open the door and glared hatred into Christina's face, which was frozen in shock.

Pearl said in an ominous whisper as she brandished an angry index finger under Christina's nose like a stiletto, "Leave my man alone, bitch! You hear me, cunt?"

Christina nodded furiously.

Pearl hissed, "I'll stomp a mud hole in your ass if you ever speak to Johnny O'Brien again. You hear me, bitch?"

Christina frantically nodded again.

Pearl leaned her face almost touching Christina's. "I'd bet you're a stone racist dog. I hope so. You'll get a shock down the line. I wish!"

Pearl slammed the door shut and went to her machine. She got in and straightened it up, then she screeched it away down the highway.

Stricken, Christina sat motionless through the horn blasts of angry motorists behind her for several light changes before she drove down the highway like an automaton.

Sweet Dreams Sour

8

FOLKS WENT into Speedy's apartment to change his clothes. He and Speedy sat on a sofa in the den and sipped a succession of whiskies and sodas as they grooved to Ray Charles records. Folks went to the bar near a window to get refills and glanced down at the street. He saw Pearl loading suitcases into the Mercury trunk.

He said, "Speedy! Look at this!"

Speedy came to the window, looked down and said laconically, "She's hitting the wind, pally."

Folks galloped from the apartment to the elevators, savagely punched at a down button. He pounded his fist into his palm as he waited, then stepped into the elevator and rode down, sprang from it and raced to the street. Pearl's car had disappeared. He got into his car and desperately tried to spot her for an hour and a half.

He drove back and went to his apartment with Speedy and found Pearl's note on the bed. He sat down heavily on the side of it. Her tears had run the ink.

He read: *"Dear Johnny, sorry to do it this way. I lost my temper and I'm so ashamed. I thought I'd be nigger crazy and strong enough to tough it with you, until things worked out for us. Be happy with your new love, Johnny. I'm chicken, I just can't compete with my competition. She's a wipe out, Johnny. And after all, she's got the edge I guess, since you both have white skins in common. I tried to make you happy. You know that. But, like you always said, "Somebody is got to lose when somebody wins." Don't forget to take your vitamins every day. Good-bye, Pearl."*

The jangle of the phone beside him on the nightstand startled him. He picked it up and said, "Hello."

He heard Kid's cold voice crackle. "Stay at home, Johnny. Trevor and I will be right over."

Fifteen minutes later Folks opened the door to Trevor and Kid. They walked into the living room and sat down with long faces.

Folks leaned forward in his chair and asked, "Something important pop up? Trouble, Pappy?"

Kid growled. "Just some nit shit trouble cunt freak, lopear! Christina was threatened on the highway by Pearl. She's distraught, in a rage and she's frozen the fix. We can't play for Bates! And our set-up is blown with a wave of your sucker ding

104

dong!"

Trevor said, "Johnny, I just can't understand how a fellow with your intelligence would let his girl tail him with so much at stake."

"Shut up, Trevor! I was stupid all right! Look Pappy, give me a chance to clear my skull. I'll come up with an angle to square the fix."

"You have to square up Christina, Johnny. Mother has put her in charge officially. Christina vowed to me that she's through with you. I know her well and I'm afraid you don't have a prayer to change her mind about anything."

"I can change her mind if I can talk to her. Trevor, arrange a meeting at the bank this week for Pappy with her. I'll show up."

Kid said, "Pipe dreams won't get it, laddie. She's too raw for that. Besides, what makes you think she'll see me?"

"I know her more than slightly too. She'll see us both, if for no other reason than to thrill herself with a cold turn down face to face. Set it up, Trevor."

Trevor shrugged, "I'll try, Johnny."

Kid and Trevor stood.

Kid said, "Laddie, you've got your sucker flaws, but you're a whiz with the fluffs. If any gee can turn Christina around, you can. You soured the fix, now sweeten it again if you value friendship." Kid slapped Folks' back and led the way from the apartment.

Disguising his voice, Folks fired a long shot and called Christina. He was told by a butler with obvious delusions of grandeur that Miss Buckmeister was indefinitely indisposed. Folks and Speedy sipped black coffee and put their heads together to plot turn-around strategy for the audience with Christina that Folks was certain he'd get.

Next day, Monday, Speedy received a call from Trevor at noon, four hours before his chief of security duties usually began. Victoria Buckmeister had gone sleepless, been traumatized the night before by phantom Nazi commandos she was certain were scaling the building outside her bedroom windows. She was demanding that only Speedy should install special locks on her windows. Immediately.

Speedy put on his uniform and got into his newly overhauled Datsun. He drove toward the Buckmeister castle situated on a granite peak in a remote section at the perimeter of the city. As Speedy drove up a forested incline he was impressed as always to view the spectacular Buckmeister white stone castle shimmering like a mammoth jewel in the sun. A security squad of his subordinates, impeccable in gold spangled uniforms and caps, swung open massive steel gates. The Datsun moved inside the estate past a gigantic black block of marble with the Buckmeister name and coat-of-arms chiseled into it in giant gothic letters.

Speedy parked and went into a one story building near the gates. It was the security forces office and the locus for weapons and the control center for a closed circuit network of tv cameras. They scrutinized, by night, the exterior and interior of the castle. By order of Trevor and Christina, a tv monitor in a private room was checked exclusively by Speedy on his four p.m. to four a.m. shift. It received the input from a camera secretly installed in suicidal Victoria's bedroom despite the presence of around the clock nurses.

Speedy took a tool kit and locks to Victoria's bedroom. He knocked. Millie, a sad faced elderly R.N., opened the door. Speedy stepped into the spacious room furnished in baroque Louis XIV style, with oil paintings of Victoria's wedding strung on the silk-covered walls. Others depicted imperial social scenes in Kaiser Wilhelm's Germany where she had been a grand dame.

Victoria was propped up on satin pillows in her canopied emperor bed. She was a pitiful sight clapping and cackling in glee as she watched a cartoon villain get his comeuppance on a preschoolers' tv show. Her hair was a snowy heap piled atop her ruined doll face. Her child-like antics, with her wrinkled, emaciated body, gave her the appearance of a spastic fetus in the satin womb of her gargantuan bed.

Christina, in a gold silk robe, was seated on the side of the bed vainly trying to feed Victoria vegetable soup from a tray across her lap. Speedy made a mental note to tell Folks that Christina was still wearing his Aztec Princess ring.

Victoria spotted Speedy as he went toward a window. "Wade, you darling!" she exclaimed, lips pursed, as she held out her bony arms.

Speedy went to her bedside leaned his face to

take her kiss on his cheek. "How are you doing, Miss Victoria?" he said as he straightened up.

"Splendidly until those monsters tried to slip in here and murder me. Please, Wade, double lock them out. They are certain to return."

He patted her shoulder. "I'll do that, Miss Victoria, and if they come back I'll send them to be Satan's pets, as my mama used to say."

Four days later, on Friday, Trevor arranged a bank meeting with Christina for Kid. The plan was that Kid would, when he kept his appointment, casually mention to the bank's security guard, whose job he owed to Kid, that his business associate would be a few minutes late. Kid requested of him that he escort Johnny O'Brien to the executive office when he arrived.

Ten minutes later, Folks drove to the bank with Speedy in the Eldorado. Folks went into the popular bank which was bustling with clients. The security guard took him to the door of Christina's office. He pushed a button and a buzzer sounded to unlock the door.

The guard swung the door open and said, "Miss Buckmeister, Mister Borenstein's associate, Mister O'Brien." The guard turned away.

Surprise and irritation shadowed Christina's face for an instant as Folks stepped into the room with a warm smile on his face. "Good afternoon, lady and gentlemen."

Trevor and Kid said, "Hello Johnny," almost simultaneously.

Christina stiffened behind her massive mahogany

desk and said coldly, "Good afternoon. I wasn't expecting you, Mister O'Brien. But now that you are here, have a seat and I will repeat to you what I have just said to Trevor and Saul." She nodded toward a gleaming gold coffee service on her desk. "Coffee, Mister O'Brien, to brace yourself for the bad news?"

He smiled thinly and shook his head. He glanced at his ring on Christina's finger.

She flushed scarlet, slipped off the ring and slid it on the desk top toward him. "Something I forgot to return, Mister O'Brien."

"Thank you," he smiled as he dropped it into his blue serge vest.

Trevor and Kid at that intimate juncture left the office.

She said evenly, "Mister O'Brien, this bank has backed its last swindle! My final answer is no! However, if you are flat broke perhaps Trevor or even I could loan you and your rabid little bird dog plane fare to your next sucker adventure. Oh, by the way, she suggested that I was racist and as such she predicted a mega shock for me. Any idea what she meant?"

Folks shrugged and smiled urbanely. "Maybe she's leading a revolution. And no thank you to welfare. I don't need it. We do need you to change your mind, to be reasonable. Saul is an old man with his life savings and energies invested in our set-up. Don't hurt him and his associates just to hurt me. Restore the fix and I'll cop a heel permanently. Be reasonable!"

Her eyes shot gray flame. "I will not change my decision! I am always reasonable with honest people."

Her hands shook as she took a cigarette from a case. Folks rose, leaned to flick his lighter to her cigarette. He leaned even closer across the desk.

He grinned lewdly and winked wickedly as he crooned, "No from you will always be unacceptable to me. You can imagine why, I'm sure. I've peeped at your hole card, humper by firelight. We will play for Mister Bates!"

Trevor and Kid entered the office and took their seats.

Christina said, "Ha! Biological encounters for me are as forgettable as rainstorms. I dare you to even play for a short con mark in this state! Please take your chair, Mister Wellington! You . . . ah . . . mouthwash makes me nauseous."

Folks reseated himself.

Trevor leapt to his feet and spilled it out. "Chris, I will not let you do this to my friends! I'm the executive in charge of deposits and withdrawls. I'll back them! I'll move the Bates money for the score. I'll see the captain and arrange the fix for the Bates play!"

Christina said contemptuously, "The captain wouldn't fix a jay-walking ticket for you now without my approval. Trevor, please sit down. My final answer to you, Trevor, to you all as before, is no."

Red-faced and deflated, Trevor left the office. Kid and Folks got to their feet and walked to the open door.

Christina followed them. "Good-bye, loser."

Folks turned. Their eyes locked for a long moment as she stared up into his bland face.

He said, "I know what you're thinking when you look at me like that."

"Tell me."

"You were thinking about the great hitch in my hips on the downstrokes."

"You conceited rectum. I was thinking you should be compelled to carry documents."

His eyebrows then took a ride. "Documents, Poontang?"

She frowned. "Don't call me that! Yes, liar. Documents to prove you've got a brain, or even a heart. You've struck out all around. Hallelujah!"

He smiled smugly. "Now you're a liar, Poontang." He started to turn away.

She seized and gripped his sleeve and said harshly, "I'm too good for you, Utah Wonder. Go back to the coal pit plantation with Little Eva. On Saturday nights, you can ditch her as you certainly will, to get a belly full of rot gut whiskey and take a five dollar bill to a two buck whore and live happily ever after!"

He stabbed an index fingernail into the tender web between the thumb and index finger of her hand clutching his sleeve. She snatched her hand away and pressed her lips against the wound like a little kid. She bombed a fist at his groin that missed as he turned his hip to catch the blow.

"You rotten bastard!"

He shaped an amused smile and turned away as she banged the door shut. Kid compulsively shook his head as they went to the street, across the sun-splashed sidewalk to the Eldorado. Folks got in next to Speedy under the wheel as Kid got in the back. He threw his head back and he closed his eyes, pressing the knuckles of his hands against his temples as Speedy pulled the car into traffic.

The Kid moaned and said, "The museum, the mansion, the ghost town set-ups are waiting. We got a mark that stands to drop a mil! But we've got no fixes to back the play. I think I'm having a stroke! I warned you she was too raw."

"Save the stroke, Pappy, for a proper occasion. We'll play for Bates. I've got the angle to turn Christina around. All Speedy has to do is get me inside the castle to make it work."

"What?"

Folks laughed. "Yeah, lopear. Who the hell else can get me in except you, the chief of security."

Kid moaned, "Have you lost your alleged mind? I just saw that wildcat try to punch off your balls. So how in the hell do you figure to turn her around?"

"I can turn that witch around. I know I can!"

Kid said, "I've laid out a bundle for the Bates play, including the production of a documentary film convincer. We're about to be ridden out of town on a rail. Is it asking too much for a hint as to what your turn around angle is for that broad?"

"Trust me, Pappy! Keep the faith. Speedy believes I'll find and punch her 'yes' button, don't you, pal?" Folks laughed.

Speedy hee-hawed. "Sure, Saul. He's got a sure-shot angle. He's going to snatch Victoria, tie me into a kidnap beef and hold the old lady for fix ransom until Christina turns around."

Folks cuffed the side of Speedy's head and knocked off his brand new hat.

Speedy replaced it on his long head and exclaimed, "My fifty buck lid!"

Folks said, "I'm so sure I can turn her around in the next two days that I'm making an appointment today with Bates to tour his ranch for sale this weekend. So Speedy, swing the castle gates wide tonight for Christina's heart throb!"

Speedy said, "Make it late, Buddy. There's a big bash at the castle tonight."

Kid said, "It can't work."

Folks said, "It will work. She's a fantasy freak. By purest chance I spun her sex tumblers to open her up. She's hooked and hot! I'm her composite living link-up, rare and secret treasure."

Kid said, "Hot to cross you."

"Draw charts on marks, Pappy. Leave the broads to me. Sure, on the surface she despises me. But that's only a gauge of Christina's underbelly of bitch dog heat and yen for me. The psychology is the same as when Mary Smith, the punishment junkie, heckles her old man until he drags her to fist alley. Afterwards, both the freaks get hyped to hump up a storm to make up.

"Christina is like that in a scaled down way. I'll play Mary Smith's old man for her. I'll corner her. I'll chastize her with my whip, and turn her around.

She'll be easy, friends. Christina can't douche me down her erotic toilet just like that. I refuse to let her sucker me out into the cold. Camille Costain did it. But never again!"

Kid mused bitterly, "Laddies, I'll have to confess, I've been a lopeared sucker for fluffs since I escaped the plow and the stink of mule farts down home in Mississippi. I was twenty before I got laid. My pappy was a racist bastard, the cruelest cocksucker slavemaster in the county, if not the state. There were six of us boys that slaved in the fields from dawn to dusk under Pappy's eye. His tyranny killed my mother. He almost beat me to death with a tow chain when he caught me shooting the breeze with a black chum I liked. I was sure I'd kill him after that, if I didn't leave. So, I sneaked away and joined a medicine show as a shill to learn the fundamentals of the con. Then the carnival flat joints. At thirty I was playing long con and hooked on fancy fluffs and bright lights, a zillion miles from those goddamn mule farts!"

Speedy said, "I'm beginning to feel lucky I blew my storm and strife."

Folks said, "Janie isn't coming back from L.A.?"

Speedy sighed. "Miss Suction Pussy got her heart heisted again by a high school beau ... called me this morning. She was sweet ... had a washboard cave. I got no beef. She's twenty-two, I'm fifty-two. I held her for a month. That's not bad for an old gee.

"But my track record with broads has always been hassled. I was just a liver-lipped Harlem orphan that rose to become a first grade detective in the Apple's bunco squad. A tramp bitch got my nose open wide enough to park a Mack truck. I wasted a pretty joker I caught banging her. Maybe I shoulda wasted her and let him slide. Did a dime in the joint before they cut me loose. Played the con in the streets to survive. Janie was the second broad that got in my bed without a sawbuck up front on the dresser. Since I got a face like the Original Man's, that ain't hard to understand."

Folks leaned back against the seat, closed his eyes and visualized Pearl beside him in his bed. An abysmal downer snared him as he realized how much he missed her. Yes, he told himself. How much I love her! Christina, the poisonous bitch! She forced herself into my life. She's to blame! His scrotum sparkled with hatred, with desire more powerful than his love for Pearl.

Christina Turn Around

9

A HALF HOUR before ten that evening, Folks packed his Aztec Billy costume and make-up kit into an overnight case and drove to the Buckmeister castle. Speedy was at the gates to receive him. He pulled the Eldorado into a parking area clogged with Mercedes, Rolls and Cadillac limousines.

Speedy whisked him into the security building and said, "You can watch the bash on a monitor. There's a coffee urn in the corner." Then he locked him in.

Folks lit a cigarette and sat down on a couch facing the bank of monitors. He intently watched the one with the image of the Buckmeister dining room. A hundred odd, formally attired men and women, most of them in control of multi national corporations, sat at a long rectangular banquet table in the luxurious room. A battery of crystal chandeliers blazed dazzling light from the high ceiling.

Crystal glassware and gold serviceware glittered on snowy damask table covering before them as their cultivated conversation hummed through the monitor. Their impressive names and titles were embossed on gold leafed place cards.

Christina was an empress vision gowned in spangled black lace at the end of the table. Trevor, distinguished, aristocratic and handsome, sat at the other end of the table. Swarms of waiters scurried in puce uniforms with chest pockets embroidered with the Buckmeister coat of arms, an ancient Buckmeister knight on steed slaying a dragon. The waiters poured champagne into crystal goblets.

Trevor stood with goblet in hand. In the hush he said, "To the guest of honor, my beloved sister, Christina."

The guests rose, aimed their faces and glasses toward Christina and sipped before they sat down.

Christina rose, with glass in hand. She smiled at a blond stringbean of a man at mid table with a perpetual dour expression on his handsome face.

. Christina said, "Ladies and gentlemen, let us toast and honor the man, the proverbial heartbeat away, the honorable Chester Wiggins, the Vice-President of the United States!"

Wiggins nodded with a meager smile as the guests stood and toasted him.

Christina said, "Please keep your feet, ladies and gentlemen. Let us now toast and honor a truly great

117

and legendary lady. My friendship with most of you, my happiness, my success is due to the influencing, the caring of one of this century's most prestigious business women . . . the Grand Dame of finance and humanity, my ailing mother. The beloved Victoria Buckmeister!"

The guests toasted, then applauded enthusiastically. They descended *en masse* toward Christina, standing smilingly to receive their warm attention and congratulations.

Folks heard a joyful cackle of triumph from the adjacent private room. Curious, he walked into the room to the monitor with the image of Victoria's bedroom. A withered octogenarian R.N. in a wilted white uniform was seated on the side of Victoria's bed watching a closed circuit image of the dining room. Victoria, propped up on pillows, picked at banquet food on a tray across her lap. She childishly clapped her hands as she stared excitedly at the screen.

The R.N. said, "Congratulations, dear Victoria. Your dream has come true for Christina. Not in twenty years have I seen you so happy."

Victoria burst into tears. She sobbed, "Ella! Thank you! Thank you so much. Ella, I'm so happy! And proud!"

Then Victoria frowned and suddenly seized the R.N.'s sleeve. She clutched it desperately as her pitiful face stared up and she said, "Ella, please! Tell me, Ella, it's true! Tell me, Ella! It's real what I saw. Tell me it's not like the other splendid things that I've only imagined. Help me, Ella!"

118

The R.N. leaned over and pressed Victoria tenderly back to the security of the pillows. She kissed her forehead and patted her hands. "Dear, it's real! You can trust me."

Victoria sighed. "Oh, thank you, Ella. Thank you so much. Oh, you precious angel, think of it! The Vice-President congratulated my baby! I'm so happy I could die this moment!"

"Yes, it is just wonderful, but you must not overexcite yourself. Please eat your dinner."

Folks watched Trevor enter the room. Trevor was still immaculate in his impeccable, formal attire as he walked to the bed. He was obviously tipsy as he plopped down heavily on the side of the bed beside his mother and Ella.

Trevor slurred, "Mother, you must release Ella now. She must get some rest."

Victoria kissed Ella. Ella rose and moved away from the bed toward the door. Trevor rose and followed her.

"Just a moment, Ella."

Ella stopped and smiled.

"You're precious, Ella. Mother is radiant this evening."

Ella said, "Yes Trevor, I'm happy she's been lucid. Rational as you and myself since early afternoon."

"Small wonder, Ella. Her bright little student grew up to pre-empt me."

Ella pressed fingers against his lips. "Now, Trevor!"

Trevor wove a little as he pressed her hands to

his cheeks. His voice trembled with emotion. He said, "Nanny, I love you. Don't ever leave us . . . me!"

Ella said, "Now, stop that, Trevor!"

"Admit it, Ella, you are the only caring mother Chris and I have had since infancy."

Ella kissed Trevor, pulled away and departed. Trevor went back to the bed. He stood for a long moment with cold eyes watching Victoria eat. Then he flopped himself full length on the bed. He rested his face on his palms and elbows as he stared at Victoria's palsied ineptitude with knife and fork.

He smiled wickedly as he said, "Careful, you clumsy prune!"

Victoria whined, "Don't call me names, you torturer. Get out!" She gagged on her food and wailed, "Trevor, get the hell out of here so I can enjoy my food."

Trevor grinned at her maliciously as she resumed eating. A bit of salad dressing dribbled down Victoria's shin as she spastically forked salad into her mouth. Trevor cocked his head from side to side like a curious robin, observing a hapless earthworm.

He clucked his tongue against the roof of his mouth, saying, "Mother! You have a blob of food on your chin. Oh! What a slob!"

He reached into the tray for a napkin. She recoiled, snatched the napkin and frantically blotted her chin clean.

Victoria's voice trembled on the rim of hysteria. "Ella! Ella! Trevor's attacking me again. Trevor, go away! I'm getting sick again. Please Trevor, go away! Ella!"

Trevor taunted, "Mother, save your breath. Ella won't be back tonight."

Victoria backhanded her fork at Trevor's face. Trevor narrowly escaped as he scuttled away across the bed. Victoria feebly attempted to hurl the tray of food. Instead, she only succeeded in dumping it atop the satin quilt.

Trevor stood beside the bed, staring down at her. He said with a smirk, "You've lost your temper, Mother, like an emotional peasant. Mother, you always flogged my ass for that, remember, Mother?" Trevor fingered his belt buckle. "What was good for the goslin is doubly good for the crazy old gander!"

Victoria cringed away. She screamed, "Ella! Ella! Help me!"

Folks saw Ella dash into the room glaring at Trevor. Trevor hurriedly left.

Folks went back to the couch as Speedy keyed in and sat down beside him. They drank coffee, and sat down beside him. They drank coffee, smoked and talked until one a.m. Then Speedy escorted him to Christina's quarters in a secluded wing of the castle. Speedy nodded his head toward Christina's bedroom door as they soundlessly moved on airy carpet past it. Folks went into a vacant guest room bathroom to put on his Aztec Billy make-up and costume.

He went to her door, kneeled and put his eye close to the key hole. She was nude with her razzle of alabaster curves showcased on the pink satin spread of her mammoth bed. She undulated her bottom on a satin pillow, with crotch agape, in the pink glow of a nightstand lamp. Her hand pushed up a long plump breast to rake her teeth across the erected Bing cherry nipple. Her eyes were shuttered as she furiously jiggled the thumb tip of her other hand against her pygmy dingus. Her tapered shiny-wet fingers alternately thrusted to disappear into her four inch cone of fat blond bush.

He silently turned the doorknob and pushed the door open, then stood at the threshold watching her as she groaned and cavorted toward climax.

He clucked and said softly, "Naughty, naughty. Our Johnny would want you punished." He undid his fly.

Her eyes popped open, her face frozen in an expression of total flabbergast as she stared at the apparition. His eyes flashed blue flame in his Rasputin visage, framed by the long platinum wig. Her lips moved mutely as she struggled to speak.

He pressed an index finger against his lips. "S-s-s-sh! I will say everything . . . do everything you want to do."

He glided toward her with a crooked urchin smile as she snatched a pearl-encrusted Derringer from an open nightstand drawer and tremulously aimed it at him as she sat on the far edge of the bed.

She gasped, "I'll kill you! Get out! Please!"

He oozed closer and jerked his hips. His ten inch monster lunged from the lair of his open fly. Her bottom lip trembled uncontrollably as she gazed

122

hypnotically at the poignant ragamuffin's member bloated with blood in the pink ambience.

She waggled the Derringer and shouted, "Please don't make me kill you! Take that back to your jigaboo bitch."

He kissed, caressed the air between them with his fingertips and crooned as he floated to the bedside, "Johnny loved Pearl, but he loves you more. He's sent her away forever."

She stared at him transfixed and he gently lifted the pistol from her hand and flung it away to the carpet.

She exclaimed, "You're insane! Please! I can't let . . . ."

He caressed her lips mute with his fingertips, then her throat and her nipples as he kneed her thighs apart. She moved her lips to protest but he leaned and smothered them with a feathery kiss. Her eyes softened doe-like as her fingertips sensuously stroked the backs of his hands caressing her ears.

She buried her face in his groin and sobbed, "Oh, you adorable maniac! Angel from the coal pits, I'm still mad about you!"

He thought, it's "prat-out" time to cinch her as he scuttled away across the carpet with a sly old face. Her eyes brimmed tears as she leapt to her feet in pursuit, and he let her catch him at the door.

She clutched him desperately to her, weeping even as she laughed uncontrollably and begged, "Please don't leave me, you gorgeous, sweet, ugly sonuvabitch!" She slipped the Aztec Princess ring from his finger and slipped it on her finger. "I love you. I can't do without you," she said as she led him to the side of the bed.

She sat down on the side of it and she yelped ecstatically as he seized her hair and yanked her head to his crotch. A torrent of hateful triumph drowned his mind. Grenades of power wobbled his knees as he watched her deep-throat his organ with feline purrs of surrender.

10

AT THE END OF THE WEEK, Folks, Trevor and Bates, the mark, driven by Speedy in a rented limousine, drove toward Nevada to tour Bates' ranch for sale.

In town, Kid's woman, Rita, the fledgling grifter in the minor role of Lance Wellington's Baroness sister, stood impatiently on the front porch of the mob's museum-mansion set-up in a secluded area of the city. She awaited arrival of a crew of back-up shills recruited for the Bates play. The spires of the pearly prop seemed ablaze in the brilliant noon sun. It appeared afloat like a gem boat in a landscaped sea of jade.

A legitimate employment agency bus labeled *Peerless Personnel Service* pulled into the parking area on the right of the showplace. A group of uniformed servants spilled out and moved toward the mansion's front door.

Rita inspected the nails and uniforms of the servants as they passed her and entered the mansion. The back-up players, costumed as titled aristocrat jet swingers, arrived and emerged from limousines. Rita was haughtily regal in her role as Lance's sister and hostess as she stood in the crystal chandeliered entrance hall of the mansion. She greeted her elegantly attired confederates.

A monocled fake count, with a sex pot brunette on his arm, approached Rita. He bent at the waist and kissed the back of Rita's extended hand. He said, "Good afternoon. How lovely you are, dear Baroness!"

Rita replied, "Count! Countess Fertig! How marvelous you both came. Countess, you are just ravishing!"

"Thank you very much, Baroness."

A heavy-set ex-convict shoplifter, with an aristocratic face and bearing, entered the hallway and approached Rita.

With a clipped English accent, Rita said, "So good to see you again, Duchess!" Then under her breath, "Myrtle, watch yourself! The servants are from a legit employment agency. Now get to the powder room and dilute your mascara."

The fake Duchess said, "How very kind of you to invite me, dear Baroness." She plucked a mote of lint off Rita's black lace dress and whispered, "Lint in the cleavage is a worst omen than playing for a blind or crippled mark." The Duchess moved on.

Flo Baumgarten, ex-pickpocket and spurious French noblewoman, approached, wearing *pince-nez* glasses perched precariously on her long aquiline nose.

She embraced Rita and gushed, "Oh Baroness, so good to see you in gorgeous living, beautiful flesh! You dear woman, I've missed you since that marvelous summer on the Riviera. Dear Baroness, thank you for inviting me. How's Lance?"

Rita said, "Lance is fine. We're all expecting his arrival shortly." Then she whispered, "Flo, your breath stinks like bootlegger mash! Deodorize your breath before the play!"

Flo whispered, "It isn't whiskey, Rita. It's gin, your favorite poison." Flo smiled and moved on.

Rita finally received the last group of the shills and moved with them into the palatial mansion.

A crew of grifter menials in coveralls feverishly hung counterfeit Old Masters on the silk-covered walls. Several of the crew went down a short flight of stairs to a high domed room, pregnant with mysticism in its lighting and decor. They pried open a huge wooden crate to reveal a compelling giant plaster replica of the Aztec Princess Statue.

Two hours later, the mob settled in drinking and chatting as they impatiently waited for Folks to lug Bates in for the play.

Speedy, in chauffeur's uniform, tooled the limousine, with Folks, Trevor and Bates on the rear seat down a dusty ranch road. The bedlam of snorting mustangs, bellowing steers and shouting cowboys rent the afternoon air. Speedy's passengers scrutinized herds of cattle grazing on seemingly endless rolling hills of green as the limo moved to the ranch exit.

Four cowpokes swung open massive oaken gates. One of them, the real ranch owner, smiled as Bates, the government undercover ace, winked at him. Speedy rolled the limo onto the highway.

Trevor, as Folks' pompous business manager-accountant Glitz, shuffled notes and examined them through heavy horn-rimmed glasses.

Folks said, "Mister Glitz, may I see your evaluation?"

Trevor gave Folks his notes.

Folks took them and studied them for a long moment. "Glitz, congratulations. Your opinion is mine."

Trevor beamed. "Thank you, Mister Wellington! I knew instantly, the property was ideal for your purposes. I will have our New York office prepare the paperwork and get an instrument drawn as a binder for your deal with Mister Bates within the next two weeks."

"Not two weeks, Mister Glitz! I want that half million dollar binder money in Mister Bates' possession within a week!"

Trevor said, "Of course. I'll fly back after I have assisted you in the acquisition of the Unhappy Virgin Relic."

"Very well, Glitz. I have acquired a spectroscope to test her authenticity when we have discovered her precise location."

Speedy turned his head back. "Mister Wellington, sir, do I proceed directly to the mansion?"

Folks said, "Gifford, I think Mister Bates wants to take in the ooh-la-la's on the Vegas strip."

Bates said, "I'll pass up the pony broads. Take me to my hotel just to slip on a tux. Then Lance, my boy, I'm raring to bust elbows with those beautiful people at your place."

Folks said, "Marvin, I'm sure they all will enjoy meeting you!"

Trevor and Folks brought Bates to the set-up mansion at twilight. He was introduced all around to the mob. After a sumptuous early dinner, they all went to the rec room to dance to the music of a country-western band. Rita magnetized Bates as expected. He hounded her for every dance. She was frazzled and grateful when the band took a break.

The crowd went to bar stools at the rec room bar. Folks and Flo, the fake French noblewoman, sat next to each other.

Flo said, "Lance, I'd just love to see your latest acquisitions of exotica."

Folks said, "That's a great idea, Erika! Perhaps the others might enjoy my collection."

Rita said, "Lance, what a fabulous idea! Let's all go!"

Folks got to his feet and led the way. He said, "Come on everybody! I'm inviting all of you to the museum."

Everybody followed him from the rec room. There was a gush of pleasure and excitement from the fake aristocrats as the group moved through the palatial set-up to the mystically lighted display of fake artifacts whose history existed only in the facile and ultra-inventive minds of the Kid and Folks. There was a carefully effected ambience here, the mystique of countless centuries with their zillion souls now entombed and keening from the rows of glass topped crypts, from the Dracula visages of statuary sentries that stalked the shadow-haunted murk.

Bates' eyes gazed ahead toward the rear of the museum. He walked over to stare at the Unhappy Virgin statue, ten feet of fierce-faced Aztec glory cast in copper-hued plaster. Bates returned to Folks' side, with the grifter troupe.

They peered into and moved past cases. Folks moved toward the giant statue to start his lecture to ignite the crossfire that would validate the statue and artifacts. Trevor paused beside a spectroscope on a dolly between a pair of the display cases. Bates stared at it.

Trevor said, "Congratulations, Mister Wellington! This is the latest in spectroscopes."

Folks said, "Yes, it's self-contained, transistorized for x-raying artifacts in remote areas."

Bates rubbed his hand across the spectroscope. "That's a mighty impressive machine you got there, Lance. Reminds me of the contraption in the hospital that took a picture of my gallstones when I had 'em took out last year."

The mob chuckled. The group moved on to stand tittering as they gazed into a display case of ancient chamber pots.

Folks pressed his index finger against the glass

above a squat brass beauty that had an intricate gold filigreed lid. He said, "Loves, in the category of portable johns, this is the crown jewel of this collection. Tireless search by my curator and field staff led to this acquisition from a Russian peasant in Siberia. She was ignorantly using this gem as a . . ." Folks paused for dramatic impact. ". . . common chamber pot! Credible legend has it that Rasputin, by hypnotic persuasion, conquered the Czarina's near terminal . . . ah, problem on that very vessel! What outcries of joy and gratitude must have shaken that Royal Chamber!"

Bates and the mob laughed.

Folks led the group to upholstered chairs arranged before a movie screen and projector, then sat at the machine. The others took their seats around him.

Folks said, "This film I'm about to show is a brief, but authentic reproduction of the events that depict the tragic dilemma of how an Aztec Princess, centuries ago, perished in a castle tower prison."

Folks turned on the projector. The room darkened. An image of the Unhappy Virgin statue appeared on the screen to start the brief documentary and Folks' narration.

Bates said, "Lance, she's flat out got Sam Houston's statue down home snookered!"

Folks launched into the first phase of the tale. "Congratulations Marvin, you have sensed her importance to me. Her story is the most fascinating of the entire collection. Unfortunately, I've had to buffer my frustrations with a plaster copy, executed from Aztec etchings. Uncounted thousands were spent over the last ten years in a fine comb search of Latin America, and recently in the Western section of this country. Dogged investigation revealed that a paranoid Aztec King had an unfortunate . . . uh, incestuous jealousy of his beautiful young virgin daughter."

The key scenes of the Unhappy Virgin's tragedy unfolded on the screen accompanied by Folks' narration. An Aztec period royal bedroom flashed on the screen. It was midnight. An ethereally beautiful young girl slumbered on an opulent bed. The room was haunted with shadows and the flickering glow of an altar candle beside the bed. Suddenly, an old man in royal robes and golden crown, eased from the shadows.

Folks narrated, "The King had decided that only he would be his virgin daughter's first lover. Insane with evil passion, the King fondled his sleeping daughter."

The King stripped off his robe and nude, he carefully slipped into bed beside the sleeping beauty. The King pulled away the bed covers. The girl's magnificent naked body gleamed. The King kissed her feet and traversed upward to her bosom. Her eyes fluttered open in alarm.

Folks said, "She awakened. She clawed and maimed the King."

On the screen the Princess violently resisted her father's assault by clawing, biting and well aimed kicks to the scrotum. The King fell prostrate on the floor as a squad of royal guards rushed into the room. The King feebly rose to a sitting position, his face lacerated and ferocious with rage. He pointed a dramatic finger at his daughter, cringing in the corner of the room and the royal guards seized her roughly. One of the guards raised his sword to decapitate the Princess, but the King struggled to his feet and seized the up-raised hands of the guard.

Folks said, "Enraged, the King planned a worse fate than death for his daughter. Imprisonment! In the castle tower! Until she agreed to lavish her royal cherry on her father, the King!"

The screen went blank for an instant before the image of the imprisoned Princess, dressed in rags and peering through a barred window appeared on the screen.

Folks went on. "The King, on her sixteenth birthday, cunningly gifted the Virgin with a be-jeweled ten foot copper statue in her image. The statue was really a spy-post for a succession of slaves, imprisoned inside the statue and watered and fed until death. The King was determined to be the Virgin's first lover."

On the screen peep holes in the Statue were suddenly filled with luminous human eyes. Through the barred windows, the ruined, hideously old face of the Princess peered pitifully.

Folks said, "In that terrible tower, loves, the Unhappy Virgin became old, ugly, and dead!"

The movie screen went blank and the group applauded as Folks rose to his feet.

Bates said, "We got a remedy back home for

skunks like that King. A long stretch in the pen."

Folks led the group to a prop relic, whose importance was indicated by its residency in a six foot case, spangled with fake gold leafing. This supposedly ancient counterpart of today's inflatable mail-order sex dolls was an expertly time-hacked mannikin. It was ostensibly constructed of Napoleon-era velvet, stuffed with early Egyptian cotton. A tattle-tale gray blob of stuffing popped from a nipple, apparently lacerated by the mannikin's famous master.

Folks started to narrate the ancient sex doll's history. "This battered little lady did much to comfort and gratify Napoleon's rather . . . ah, odd sex play on lonely Elba. It is even said that Napoleon, in an erotic fury . . ." Folks paused.

A fake grifter, disguised as a Western Union employee, entered the museum and gave Folks a telegram. The grifter said, "Telegram, Mister Wellington."

Folks took it and said, "Thank you," at the same time signing for it. The delivery grifter departed with a tip. Folks' hand shook as he tore open the telegram. As he read, his face became radiant with excitement.

His voice trembled. "Loves! I've hit the Unhappy Virgin jackpot!" He excitedly waved the telegram. "This telegram brings me the electrifying confirmation that an ailing old prospector in this area known as Aztec Billy is in possession of the priceless original Unhappy Virgin statue!"

The guests moved in and congratulated Folks enthusiastically. They moved into the living room to drink champagne:

After several goblets of bubbly, Bates performed on all fours his proud impression of his favorite Angus Bull in rabid heat. The mob applauded wildly as he snorted and pawed the carpet in courtship of an imaginary bovine sexpot. His moon face was sweat shiny and his tuxedo rumpled as he collapsed on the sofa beside Rita. She mopped the sweat off his brow with a handful of tissues.

Rita said, "Marvin, that was the most marvelous animal impression I've ever seen. You were super great."

Bates said, "Then kiss me, Baroness!"

He grabbed the back of her head and pulled her mouth down to his. Rita's face deformed with revulsion and resentment. The mob howled with genuine amusement at the fledgling grifter's anguish.

Bates fell into an apparent drunken stupor at midnight and the mob put him to bed in a guest room. Next day at twilight, he insisted, as the mob knew he would, on going to the ghost town set-up with Folks and Trevor to check out the rumor that Aztec Billy was indeed in possession of the authentic Unhappy Virgin statue. Speedy drove them in the limo, pulling the spectroscope on a trailer.

Folks said, "Mister Glitz, examine the statue immediately."

When they arrived, Kid, with red tinted face and headband to control his long, coarse black wig, was in the death shack with High Pockets Kate, in the role of Mrs. Peabody, ghost town buff staring down at expired Billy, played by the grifter trooper. The statue loomed above the shack.

Trevor and Speedy dollyed the spectroscope to the statue at the rear of the death shack. Bates followed Folks into the death shack as Kid wrung his hands and covered Billy's face with a tattered blanket.

Kid said, "I'm Jimmy Dancing Rain. I'm afraid poor Billy, my brother, has passed away. Poor black sheep Billy shed his sweat in a hundred gold camps, died a pauper with only a delirium of riches."

Folks said, "I'm Lance Wellington. This is Mister Bates, a business friend. My sympathy to you, sir, but I am interested in the Unhappy Virgin statue owned by your late brother."

Kid frowned. "I'm not about to sell Billy's property piecemeal, Mister Wellington. Oh, by the way, this lady is Mrs. Peabody."

Folks and Bates smiled and nodded.

Trevor entered the shack. He whispered into Folks' ear. "It's authentic! Ten points genuine!"

Bates was leaning to hear.

Folks said, "Mister Dancing Rain, I would like to bid for Billy's property."

Kid said, "Well, let's go to the stable with Mrs. Peabody and take a look at the bulk of Billy's artifacts."

Kate's face creased with aggravation.

Kid said, "You seem tense, Mrs. Peabody. Are you still upset at my decision not to sell this ghost town piecemeal?"

Kate pretended to be chastened. She said, "Of

course not, Mister Dancing Rain. But Aztec Billy promised me last week that he would sell me separately all the figurines in the relic shack. Of course, I have no reluctance to bid for the ghost town itself. It would make a fabulous museum!"

They followed Kid from the death shack, and Folks, Trevor and Bates lagged outside as Kid and Kate entered the adjacent stable lit by lamplight. Speedy sat in the limo smoking a cigarette as he listened to radio jazz.

Folks said, "Mister Glitz, are you certain of the statue's authenticity?"

Trevor said, "Absolutely!"

"Splendid! I must have that statue!" He walked into the stable followed by Trevor.

Aztec Billy groaned to halt Bates. He went into the death shack, pulled back the blanket and leaned his face close to Billy's.

Billy rolled his eyes to the top of his head. He choked out, "Ten million . . . cash!"

Bates said, "This is Jimmy, your brother, Billy. Where is the money?"

Billy death rattled and whispered, "Virgin . . . 'neath her feet." Billy sighed and died.

Bates covered his face and went to the statue at the rear of the death shack. He aimed the spectroscope down to see the dozen odd fat duffel bags crammed into the hole in the ground. The bags on top were gaped open to reveal a layer of real money. Folks watched Bates through a peephole in the rear of the stable as Bates feigned excitement and hurried away toward the stable.

Inside the stable, Kid stood inside an ancient wagon. Folks nodded his head as he came to the wagon to start the play. Then Kid banged a walking cane against the top of the wagon.

Kid said, "For the land, buildings and their contents, I'm bid two hundred and fifty thousand . . . once!" Kid struck the wagon with the cane.

Bates entered the stable with his briefcase beneath his arm. He stood close to Folks and Trevor, radiant with fake tension.

Kate said, "Fifty thousand!"

Kid said, "Mrs. Peabody bids three hundred thousand!"

Folks said, "Three hundred fifty thousand!"

Kate said, "Mrs. Peabody bids four hundred thousand!" Kid turned toward the Folks' trio.

Trevor stage whispered into Folks' ear. Bates leaned close to hear. "Mister Wellington, bidding is rather steep, don't you think? After all, it's just a rare statue, stripped of its jewels."

"Mister Glitz, I'm not about to quit. I'm driving Mrs. Peabody out!"

Kids' cane struck the top of the wagon bed for the second time. He said, "I'm bid four hundred and fifty thousand twice!" He banged his cane against the wagon bed.

Folks shouted, "One hundred thousand!"

Kid said, "Mister Wellington bids five hundred and fifty thousand dollars!"

Kate stuck out her chin defiantly. She darted a baleful glance toward the Folks' group. She said stoutly, "Mister Dancing Rain, I bid a hundred thousand more!"

Kid turned toward Folks. Folks fidgeted, glanced at Trevor. Kid struck the cane against the bed of the wagon.

"Six hundred and fifty thousand once . . . six hundred and fifty thousand twice. All valid bids must be backed by cash or its equivalent."

Folks said, "Fifty thousand!"

Trevor whispered into Folks' ear. Bates leaned in to eavesdrop. "Mister Wellington, as your business manager I must caution you . . . ."

Kid said, "Mister Wellington has bid seven hundred thousand . . . once!" Kid thudded his cane against the wagon.

Trevor continued, ". . . that you have available to you for this transaction only seven hundred and fifty thousand dollars in immediate liquid cash. Any bid beyond three quarters of a million will automatically eliminate you as a viable bidder under Mister Dancing Rain's rules of auction."

Kate said, "Seven fifty!"

Kid said, "Mrs. Peabody bids three quarters of a million dollars . . . once!" He struck his cane against the wagon, then banged it again. He turned inquiringly toward the Folks' trio. "Three quarters of a million . . . twice!"

Trevor whispered to Folks and Bates leaned in. "She's outbid your capacity to acquire the Unhappy Virgin."

"Mister Glitz, I must have that statue! Request of Mister Dancing Rain some kind of a remedy for me."

Kid intoned, "Seven hundred and fifty thousand for this ghost town and the contents therein."

Trevor said, "Mister Dancing Rain! I request that you alter the rules a bit to permit Mister Wellington to liquidate certain holdings to facilitate his continued bidding."

Kid lowered his cane. "How long will that take?"

Folks said, "Only twenty-four hours. I can have a million dollars in cash from New York transferred by draft to a local bank."

Kate dashed to the wagon. She shook a furious index finger at Kid. "Mister Dancing Rain, under threat of lawsuit, make no such concession to Mister Wellington. I, too, am near the end of my capacity to bid." She waved a checkbook. "I demand that you honor my last bid as official and final!"

Bates whispered into Folks' ear. "Hang in there, Lance, my boy! We can snooker the Peabody broad. I've got a million in liquid cash to back you."

Folks said, "Just a moment. One moment please, Mister Dancing Rain!"

The Folks' trio huddled.

Kate said, "Mister Dancing Rain, I demand that you close the bidding!"

Folks said, "Mister Glitz, how do you interpret Marvin's proposal?"

Trevor frowned. "It's unique . . . perhaps not legally viable for your best interest, Mister Wellington."

Bates laughed. "Not viable, Mister Glitz, for Lance? I'll buy the land and make a gift of the Unhappy Virgin. What do you say to that?"

140

Trevor's face was a mask of humble remorse. "Please, Mister Bates, forgive my . . . ah, misinterpretation of your motives. Mister Wellington, your decision is obvious."

Folks said, "Marvin, Mrs. Peabody is all yours."

Bates said, "Mister Dancing Rain! Mister Wellington has just given me permission to bid as his furrogate in my own name. Nine hundred thousand dollars!"

Kid said, "Mister Wellington, is that true?"

Folks nodded.

Kate shouted, "Mister Dancing Rain, I warn you! I shall contest this farce in the courts!"

Kid struck his cane against the wagon bed. "Mister Bates bids nine hundred thousand dollars . . . Once!" He struck the wagon again. "Nine hundred thousand . . . twice!" Kid raised the cane to strike the wagon bed for a third and final time before Bates' bid was final.

Kate said, "Nine hundred and fifty thousand!"

Kid's cane struck for the third time an instant after Kate's hair-breath bid.

Bates smiled triumphantly in Kate's direction as he moved away several feet to his briefcase atop an old anivil. He turned his back to shield his actions as he opened the case, then stamped $1,000,000 on a presigned check from an array of print devices inside the case.

He turned back and said, "I bid a million dollars, Mister Dancing Rain!"

Kid struck the wagon. He said, "This property is going at one million dollars to Mister Bates.

Once!" He struck the wagon. "Twice!" He struck the wagon again.

Kate was shocked and livid with rage.

"Thrice!" Kid struck the bed of the wagon for the third and final time to close out the bidding.

Kate descended on Kid. She snatched his cane, smashed it into splinters across the wagon. "You crooked Indian, slice of dung! I'll rescind this auction in court!"

Kid sputtered as he ignored Kate and waved a pair of documents at Bates. "Now, Mister Bates, your purchase cash, or its equivalent."

Bates stepped forward and extended the check. "This is a cashier's check issued to me for purchase of a parcel of Oregon land I own. This is a completely negotiable instrument."

Kid took the check as Kate craned her neck over the wagon top to peer at it. Kid smiled. "This instrument is indeed the equivalent of cash, Mister Bates. It's payable to bearer."

Kate said harshly, "See you in court, Mister Dancing Rain!" She turned and stomped from the stable.

Kid handed Bates a pair of documents. "Your quit-claim deed and bill of sale to the property, Mister Bates. Congratulations!"

Bates grinned as he took the documents from Kid. Then Bates said, "You're a remarkable man, Mister Saul Borenstein, alias Vicksburg Kid."

Bates drew a magnum pistol from a shoulder holster and fired several rapid, booming rounds into the stable ceiling. Folks, Trevor and Kid were

142

paralyzed with shock as they stared slack-jawed at Bates as he waved his open wallet under their eyes. A badge pinned to the leather was inscribed *U.S. Treasury Department.*

A U.S. Marshal's prison van rumbled down the ghost town's main street, screeching to a halt across the doorway of the stable, trapping the occupants. A dozen business-suited federal agents leapt from the van and dashed into the stable. Kate was apprehended as she turned on the headlights of her rented Chevrolet. The task force seized the con players and handcuffed them.

As the group moved through the stable door, Bates spoke to Folks with his natural, crisp New England accent. "John O'Brien, alias Utah Wonder, I actually grew to like you, and even admire your intelligence. What a pity you didn't emply your extraordinary talents toward legitimate goals. I'm sorry to have to do this, son!"

The fake trooper in the Billy role and the mob were loaded into the steel-grilled van, which then went down the bleak main street toward the highway.

11

THE CON MOB'S BONDSMAN posted their bond next day after hasty hearings before a U.S. Commissioner in the Federal Building. Trevor, Folks, Speedy and Kid went directly from a Government wing of cells in county jail to Kid's apartment for a conference with the mob's attorney, the city's fabled fixer. They were somewhat heartened to find only a brief account of their arrest in the newspaper on page six. They drank cocktails and snorted coke in the den, as they impatiently waited.

Folks called Christina and was told by the haughty butler that she was indisposed.

The lawyer arrived an hour late. He flopped his short, fat bulk into a chair and mopped his florid face with a handkerchief from the breast pocket of his five hundred dollar suit. Rita served him a frosty daquiri as his audience leaned forward to get his prognosis of the future.

He said, "Trevor, I've worked out a deal with the U.S. attorney relative to the alleged Federal Bank Act violations involving the illegal movement of swindle victim's money during the past year by the Buckmeister Bank. I convinced the government that your sister had no knowledge whatsoever of your illegal transactions." The lawyer paused to sip his drink.

Trevor quavered. "Mister Greenberg, I can't handle a prison term."

Greenberg smiled as he waved his hand as if swatting away an invisible insect. "You won't be required to. It has been arranged that you will enter a plea of guilty and be placed on probation . . . in quiet proceedings, thanks to the support of powerful Buckmeister friends in Washington."

Trevor sagged back on the sofa with relief as Greenberg lit a cigar.

Kid said, "And what about the rest of us, Max?"

Greenberg gave Kid a level look. "Saul, the arrangements I have made for you and your . . . ah, associates are not idyllic. Neither are they catastrophic. Thanks to the zeal and overeagerness of the government's Mister Bates, which led to his error in making his arrests before he let you clear the check and pocket the money from the score, a conspiracy charge to violate the Bank Act is not considered by the U.S. attorney. Too, I hinted that entrapment could be a defense.

145

"However, the U.S. attorney does have Bank Act conspiracy evidence against you and your associates involving a half dozen other of your . . . ah, customers. There are state charges relative to a Mister Stilwell. I have an agreement with the government and Captain Ellis, of bunco, that all charges, Federal and local, will be squashed. Fortunately for us, they obviously want the whole affair quietly resolved."

Kid shook his head dubiously. "Max, all charges dropped just like that? I suspect a double cross!"

Greenberg smiled. "They're on the level with me. You see, Saul, the stipulations of my agreement with them is that you make full restitution to Mister Stilwell and fifty percent reimbursment to the others fleeced by the Unhappy Virgin game. This and your exit from the state must be accomplished within seventy-two hours."

Kid leapt to his feet. "Max, your deal will break me!"

"I'm sorry Saul. It's the best I could do under the circumstances." Greenberg got to his feet. "Come into the office in the morning to arrange the restitutions." He patted the Kid's shoulder as he left the room.

Folks said, "Saul, cheer up. I'm engaged to a walking mint, remember? I'll get a chunk of the restitution dough from Christina so you won't have to tap out. It's not doomsday. We'll set up our store some place. Maybe we can fix in the Apple or even in Denver."

Kid mumbled, "Yeah, maybe."

146

Folks and Speedy got to their feet. They walked to the front door when a terrible thought hit Folks. He had been fingerprinted! And besides that, Bates most certainly had an F.B.I. dossier on him. That dossier would reveal that he was black. He couldn't risk Christina's reaction, unmarried, if she found out.

Captain Ellis was her most likely and immediate source of discovery, he thought. He'd have to persuade, bribe, the captain to keep the secret, even change or excise his racial designation on all F.B.I. documents in the captain's possession.

Folks picked up a phone in the entrance hall, called Captain Ellis' office and was told he was off for the day. He called the captain's home. The line was busy.

Folks and Speedy went to the Eldorado and drove to the captain's neat beige stucco house in the suburbs. Folks parked in front of it, got out and went down a long walk bisecting a wide expanse of velvet lawn. The captain, in floppy straw hat and faded coveralls, was on his knees in the blistering sun with chopping shears at a scarlet profusion of rosebushes ringing the front of the house.

Folks heard the captain's four children laughing and the flat thudding of their hands against a volley ball in the backyard. The captain's sloe-eyed blonde wife was seated on the front porch rocking an infant in a crib. Her lips moved and the captain turned and squinted in the sun as Folks reached him. He pushed back his straw hat, irritation and

147

surprise flickering across his beet red, sweaty face.

Folks said, "Good afternoon, Captain. Beautiful roses."

The captain said coolly, "Thanks, Utah Wonder, from Chicago's southside. Are you drunk?"

"Why no, Captain. I . . . ah . . . ."

"Well, what the hell *is* your problem that you and that other darky would come here to my home with the city lousy with government agents?"

Folks said, "It's an emergency, Captain. Your help is needed. Bad!"

The giant captain stood, his dark eyes hard as he towered over Folks. "Count your blessings, boy, that you got a floater instead of the joint. I'm not doing any more favors for anybody, including the Vicksburg Kid. Tell him that!"

Folks said, "Look Captain, Kid didn't send me. You found out I'm a black man. Captain, all I want is that you will keep it a secret. Please! I'll pay, Captain!"

The Captain smiled cruelly. "Why, boy?"

"It's personal. I can't tell you, Captain."

"Then I'll tell you what your motive is. You're out to con and bag Christina Buckmeister and her fortune. Boy, I can't help you make your criminal dreams come true to the detriment of my fine white friends. No!" The captain dropped to his knees and continued to chop the shears at the rose bushes.

Folks turned away for a few steps, came back. He said, "Captain, you're wrong about my intentions. We love each other . . . we're engaged. Does that mean anything to you?"

The captain's wife left the porch and stood anxiously watching them.

"Haw! Haw! Not a goddamn thing! Forget your pipe dream, boy. Last night I sent Miss Buckmeister, by special messenger, a copy of the F.B.I. dossier on you. Now, blow before I arrest you and throw you in the shit house where you belong!"

Folks stared hypnotically at a sharp, gleaming hoe at his feet. His hands twitched wildly with the powerful urge to sink the blade into the back of the captain's neck. But he tore himself from the scene and jerkily, like a somnambulist, staggered to the car in a crimson haze of murder lust.

Shortly after he got home his rage and misery were compounded by the arrival of a messenger from Christina with his ring. Without even a note of severance.

12

FOLKS SAT SNORTING COKE on a couch in the living room of his furnished apartment at six in the evening after his visit to Captain Ellis' home. His packed bags were stacked at the front door. He and Speedy had decided to team up and play the short con together until Kid could find a city to fix for the long con.

He stared at a pair of Pearl's blue-furred house slippers abandoned beneath a chair. Loneliness and a bleak sense of loss tore at him. Christina had done him in, all right, he thought. Then he smiled ruefully as he realized that he had set the trap for himself with his reparations plot for Christina.

He had overcome, he thought, the compulsive urge to force a confrontation with Christina to make her tell it like it was face to face. He was irritated and frustrated that he had permitted her to sever their affair in such a coldly impersonal way, by chippie long distance really. After all, he bitterly thought, he hadn't blown her and his dream because she had tipped to the truth that he despised her. She had simply discovered that he was a nigger. That galled him.

The chimes sounded and he let Speedy in. They went to sit on the couch.

Speedy said, "Well, I sold the Datsun for what I paid for it. Guess I'll finish packing so we can split the trap."

"Yeah, I'll take the first shift under the wheel."

Speedy snorted a blow of coke and left for his apartment. Folks slipped out of his robe and pajamas and into a comfortable leisure suit for the highway. He packed the robe and pajamas into a bag and walked across the hall into Speedy's apartment, sat on the side of the bed as Speedy wound up his packing. They were leaving the apartment when the living room phone rang. They stared at it for five rings before Speedy picked up.

His jaw dropped as he gave Folks a look. He said, "Hello Miss Buckmeister. Just a moment, I'll go across the hall to see if he's in."

Folks' heart jumped rhythm at the possibility that he still had a shot at her.

Speedy put his hand over the receiver and shook his head as he whispered, "You want to talk to her? I got bad vibes."

Folks said, "I'm curious to hear the tale," as

he took the receiver and said calmly, "Hello Christina, how are you?"

She said, "Utterly miserable! Can you forgive me?"

"For what?"

"Johnny, you're bitter and it's my fault. I found out about your true background. Everything! It was a terrible shock as you must understand. I was angry because you had lied again, deceived me again. I'm sorry, so sorry I reacted like a provincial bumpkin. I don't deserve it, but please Johnny, forgive me! I'm still mad about you. Oh God, how I've missed you. Please come to me immediately so I can apologize and really explain how I feel. And I want your ring back. I've even arranged to lift your floater."

He struggled past his hoodlum ego to let his con man paranoia suspect her pitch. He was a fanatical student of human nature and there was a glaring gap in her pitch that disturbed him. It had not contained even a mild bit of female recrimination, despite the fact of her admitted shock and injury.

He said, "Angel face, I won't be free to come immediately. I'll call you within the hour to let you know when I'll be free. Pull yourself together, darling. I still love you."

"Johnny, you're so precious to reassure me. I'll be waiting for your call. Thank you, Sky Eyes." She hung up.

Folks put the receiver on the hook as Speedy said, "Let's hit the highway for Chicago, man!" He picked up his bags and followed Folks into his apartment.

Speedy yanked Folks' phone from the wall and said, "I'm gonna pee on myself if that phone rings and we pick up to the captain or a "G" man. Let's give the impression you've split town until I can drag you out."

Folks sat on the sofa with an intensely thoughtful face.

Speedy stood, with bags in hand, staring at Folks. "It's some kind of cross. She's creaming for revenge, pal."

Folks said irritably, "I thought of that, Speedy. But, what if that chart is off target? What if she's on the level? Look what I blow!"

Folks stroked the stubble of beard on his chin and got to his feet. "I need a shave," and he got his leather bound shaving kit from a bag at the door. He went into the bathroom and plugged in his shaver. He frowned at Speedy's reflection behind him in the doorway as he whittled off his stubble. Speedy followed him, picking up his bags, as he went back to the living room and packed the shaving kit.

Folks picked up his bags and said, "Let's go."

Speedy heaved a sigh of relief as he followed Folks down the hallway to the elevators. Going down, Speedy said, "I was worried about you making that call."

Folks smiled grimly. "Well, don't stop worrying. I'm going to the castle to check her out without the call. Speedy, you're forgetting there's a score of millions at stake."

Speedy shook his head in helpless exasperation as they reached the main floor. They threw their keys on the counter of the absent manager's desk and went to the underground garage. Folks pulled the Eldorado to the street, drove through the night and turned off the highway into the castle's access road.

Caught in the glare of headlights was Trevor, in a silk robe, frantically waving his long arms at the bottom of the Buckmeister hill. He raced down the road to the Eldorado as Folks braked it to a stop, and stuck his wild face through the driver's window. He panted, "Johnny, you can't go up there!"

Folks studied Trevor's face, told himself Trevor's anxiety was natural for a racist bent on protecting his sister from reconciliation with a nigger.

Folks said, "Why, Trevor? I've got an invitation from Christina."

"Johnny, I'm your friend. Please don't keep your appointment with Chris. I tried to call you to warn you."

"About what, Trevor?"

Trevor averted his eyes. "Well, Johnny . . . I'm ashamed to say it . . . but Chris, well, she's not herself. She's, uh, she's out to destroy you!"

"How, Trevor?"

Trevor spilled it out. "The security people, all the servants have been dismissed for the evening. Johnny, the castle is deserted except for Chris and Mother and Captain Ellis, with two detectives!"

Folks exclaimed, "Captain Ellis?"

"Yes, he and the others are hidden in a guest

room in Chris's wing. Johnny, don't go up there!"

Folks studied every plane and angle of Trevor's distressed face. He decided that Trevor had to be on the square. Or the most accomplished thespian who ever walked the planet.

"You've convinced me, friend. Thanks!"

He shook Trevor's hand, U-turned the Eldorado and drove to the highway for Chicago.

13

SPEEDY WAS AT THE WHEEL of the Eldorado when Chicago's skyline carnival of lights popped ablaze like the jewel case of a colossus. Folks was sprawled on the rear seat with his eyes closed against spears of light barraged by car headlamps.

Speedy said, "Look at that night-glow bitch, dap and looking good, winking her neon pussy to greet us V.I.P.'s."

Folks sat up, gazed at the spectacle. He climbed over the seat to drop down beside Speedy. He yawned, "Yeah pally, she's flashy, a stone tramp with funky armpits, dirty drawers and crabs."

Folks lit a bomber of grass. He sucked on it, then passed it to Speedy. Nat "King" Cole's poignant "Nature Boy" oozed from the radio. An aristo-

cratic-looking blonde in a Porsche drew up beside
the Eldorado on Folks' side at a stoplight on the
city's Outer Drive. She hooded her eyes and smiled
wickedly at Folks, shaped "cocksucker" with rosebud lips when he gave her the rectal salute with his
middle finger. He thought about Trevor and
Christina as Speedy pulled away on the green light.
He chuckled.

Speedy said, "Lay that humor on me to cheer
me up."

"I was wondering if Trevor could be, after all,
the most accomplished actor on the planet. There's
a long shot that the student conned me."

Speedy exclaimed, "Man, that ain't humorous.
Please don't downer me. You scare me, pal."

"I was shucking and jiving. I'm convinced Trevor
laid it out on the square . . . I think. But what if
she was playing stink finger up there? Alone?"

They laughed.

Speedy said, "Now, that's funny, man. Not ha
ha funny, but kooky funny. You know, like,
'Please Warden, hurry and let me sit in that chair.
I got a boil on my ass. I can't stand the pain!' "

The Eldorado whispered down the Drive toward
the black southside. Alongside the Drive, Lake
Michigan swirled and rippled like an endless ebonic
ribbon in the bellows of hooligan winds whose
fury seemed to jiggle the stars.

They checked into a clean hotel suite on Martin
Luther King Drive on the black mid-southside near
Forty-Seventh Street. The fox-faced, skeletal bell
captain, an old friend of Folks' and one of Blue

Howard's former short con partners, embraced Folks at the desk. He waved his underling bell-man away from the luggage, put it on a cart and showed them into the fourth floor suite.

Folks said, "Jake, I gotta tell you again, what a pleasure it is to see you again. This is Speedy, my partner."

The old man grinned and shook Speedy's hand. "Glad to meet you, Speedy. I know you gotta know you hooked up with the greatest there is and was."

Speedy screwed up his face doubtfully, then winked at him. "Sure, Jake, maybe he'll be after he plays with me for awhile."

They laughed.

Folks said, "Jake, how's the town?"

"Stinking like a two buck 'ho and hot as jasper pussy. That's why I moved my game inside this hotel five years ago. I'm too old to psyche up for a bit in the joint." He leaned in, lowered his voice to whisper. "You remember Theodore, my nephew?"

Folks nodded.

The old man pulled a crisp hundred dollar bill from a pocket of his lavender monkey suit. "It's the best 'queer' I've ever gandered," as he passed it to Folks.

Folks examined it, reversed it, whistled in amaze-ment at the perfection of the bill as he passed it to Speedy.

Speedy took it to a two hundred watt table lamp, examined it and exclaimed, "Shit, Jake!

I've pushed some fine 'queer' and this tops all I've ever handled. There are bank tellers who couldn't tip to this beauty. The only flaw is an almost microscopic fuzziness in a pinpoint section of the great seal. If you've got a bale of this, you can dump it wholesale and take a long, sweet vacation."

Jake said, "Theodore boosted a suitcase full of 'C' notes and fifties from the trunk of a car in one of them underground garages in the Loop the week before the rollers wasted him burgling a clothing store last month." He took the 'C' note from Speedy and said, "You or Folks know a safe connection that would take it all?"

Speedy said, "What do you want for it?"

"For fast turnover, I'll take ten cents on the dollar."

Speedy said, "How patient are you?"

"I think you mean how long I'll have it in hand. Well, I get my vacation in a few weeks, in September. I'm going to look up some people in New Orleans that I'm pretty sure will take it or steer me to a sale."

Speedy said, "Fine Old Timer, I'll only need a couple of weeks to sound out some people in the Apple and then in L.A. We'll talk then."

Folks said, "Jake, any of the old gang still knocking around?"

"Yeah, a few. Old man One Pocket is still trimming suckers at the old poolroom. Precious Jimmy was on the turn to get rich as cream with a southside chicken shack. But he got his nose open for craps and blew his joint to a craps magician. Now he's just a flunky manager of the joint. What's left of our old gang hang out at the old poolroom."

Then Folks' face tightened. "And what about Dot McGee, Jake?"

Jake laughed. "You can relax. Your old enemy is retired from the bunco squad. He's a private eye, got an office on the westside." Jake shook hands, turned down Folks' sawbuck and left the suite.

Folks said, "Partner, if you were serious with Jake about that bundle of 'queer,' count me out."

Speedy laughed. "Partner, I was serious. If I can make the right connection in the Apple, I'll dump that load for thirty or forty cents, maybe even fifty cents on the dollar for that great stuff. I don't mind counting you out of that deal, partner."

They unpacked their bags, hung their garments in the closets of their bedrooms. They showered, dressed themselves immaculately in blue silk leisure suits, Gucci loafers and snowy sports shirts. They called room service for filets and a jeroboam of Mumms' to celebrate their change of cities and to toast the future.

Folks called the Vicksburg Kid at the Apple's Sherry Netherlands as promised, to report his safe arrival in Chicago. He gave Rita his phone number for the absent Kid.

Folks rose from a living room easy chair, glanced at his watch as he went to a front window overlooking Martin Luther King Drive. He stared down at the heavy Saturday night rush of cars on the wide drive.

"Whatta say, Speedy, to some air to taste a

slice of the flavor of the town?"

Speedy got up from the sofa. "Sure, soon as I can brush my teeth and throw on a dash of cologne. I don't like lugging our bankrolls in the street. Wish we had a good stash." He went to the bathroom.

Folks smoked a cigarette until he returned, then went to the bathroom mirror to comb his hair and brush his teeth. He noticed a hair-line crack at the top of the mirrored cabinet over the face bowl. He got a beer can opener from the tiny kitchen, then took it to the cabinet and carefully inserted the tip into the crack against the metal edge of the cabinet. He pulled. It moved out from the plaster wall an inch. He put the opener tip to the bottom edge of the cabinet and pulled it out an inch. Then he used his hands to pull the unit from the wall and saw several inches of extra space in the hole. He and Speedy stashed their bankrolls inside, except for a few "C" notes. They pressed the cabinet snuggly against the wall and the crack was invisible.

They left the suite and went to the Eldorado parked in front of the hotel.

As Folks pulled into traffic, he said, "We'll just cruise until things start happening in the clubs."

"Good idea. Maybe I can get my jones greased when the super foxes ease from cover."

Folks swooped in the Eldorado like a masochistic homing pigeon to the dilapidated tenement apartment building where he and his mother, Phala, had existed before a hang rape pushed his alcoholic mother into the abyss of gibbering madness. He stared up at the window of their hovel where they

161

had lived when he was a teenager. He remembered the night when he had bloodied his hands smashing the glass case, containing her G-stringed image, on the facade of a ghetto cabaret.

Blindly, he made it to the front of their building. There were exactly twenty-six steps to their door. He had stood there for a long time gazing at the first of those tragic twenty-six. He knew she'd be up there at the mirror. Her greeting would tear at his insides. He'd hear the whiskey slur in her voice. The thickness of that slur was always the measure of the emptiness of the always-present fifth of Old Crow Whiskey. He went slowly up the stairs to the front of the door, twisted his key in the lock and walked into the apartment.

Her eyes were more tragic than ever in the mirror. Her greeting was thick and flat with Old Crow. She said, "Hi babee. How is Mama's tall, pretty sweetheart?"

The sight of her and his love and pity kept his bitter, angry thoughts from his voice. He held his gashed palms away from her, afraid to let her suspect what violent emotion had exploded inside him down there on the street, and not wanting her to drink any more than she had. He walked to her and kissed her on the crown of her head.

"I'm okay, P.G. How are you doing?"

He moved past her into the bathroom and cleaned out the slivers of glass from the punctures in his palms. His wounded palms tingled as he sat on the couch and watched her put on her dancer's face.

She turned her head toward the bottle of Old Crow on the dresser top and bent her head down toward the bottle. Her eyes were filmy as she stared at the dapper crow on the paper label.

She said, "Now listen, old black nigger crow. Ain't no use to roll your wicked eyes at me. I ain't young and tender any more. But you still ain't got a chance. You too black. If you white, you right. If you light, stick around. But if you black, get back. Way back."

Folks got up from the couch, eased the door open and went out carefully. He cried all the way to a chum's house.

Now he gripped the steering wheel, oblivious to Speedy beside him as he remembered the old bar porter who told him of his mother's gang rape. He had said:

"Johnny, your mama sure had a beautiful angel face. She were that pleasing color of them half-chink gals that got white pappies. I were the bar porter in that cabaret where she danced until I got fired for nipping from the bar bottles. She used to talk about your pa. To the end, she thought he were coming back to her. She were my friend.

"She used to slip me coins for my wine when I couldn't ketch up to Blue. All them no-account nigger hustlers and winos around Thirty-ninth and Cottage was just aching to fool around with Phala. But she'd put her pretty nose in the air and pass 'em like the dirt they was.

"They knowed she'd married a white man and they hated her proudness. Oh son, I could have saved her from those sinful imps. But I were stinking drunk in the lobby of the flea-bag where they abused her."

He stopped talking to wipe at his tears with his sleeve. The bar porter had continued, "It's a awful story. Everybody on them streets know'd what happened to your mama that morning. One of them slick hustlers eased up beside her at the bar just before closing time.

"Phala was drinking and tired. She didn't see the pill go in her glass. Two of them dirty niggers carried her out to the back door of the flea-bag across the street. They had rented a back room on the alley for the night. They say that cold-hearted nigger what owned the cabaret just grinned when she were carried out. He were glad because she'd never let him have her.

"When them devils finished they rotten fun, they went in them streets for blocks around. They told all the tramps and winos about your beautiful mama laid helpless and naked in that room. They say them dogs went in and out of there until daybreak.

"I were sobering up in a chair near the lobby window. I heard the pitiful screams of a woman. Then your mama came running by. She were naked as the day she were born. Her belly and thighs was caked white with jism. She were cutting herself bloody with her fingernails. I guess she were trying to scrape them niggers' filth off her. She had woke up and know'd by the stink what had happened.

"I ain't never going to forget her face. Johnny,

her eyes was twice bigger and she tored hunks of hair from out her head. I stumbled to my feet to ketch her. But she were running too quick. The last I seen, she were going down Cottage Grove, screaming her heart out.

"The Lord is surely just, though. The sneaking nigger who put that pill in her glass got his throat cut the week after. Forgive me, son, for not being in shape to save her."

To break Folks' trance of misery, Speedy said, "Say man, this spot is so exciting I can't stand it. Let's ride some."

Folks answered, "Partner, drive us to a drink. Please!" as he got out of the car and went to enter on the other side.

Speedy slid beneath the wheel and pulled the car away.

14

THEY PARKED and went into a small piano bar two blocks away on Cottage Grove Avenue. They sat at the crowded bar for a half dozen double Scotches apiece, occasionally glancing at a sepia Liberace thumping the keyboard of a battered piano on a dime-sized platform. He glittered in a gangrened silver suit of sequins, lisping obscene ballads with faggy gyrations of his blue-wigged Dracula head.

They left the bar and crisscrossed the car-clogged southside streets until Folks spotted a tall grey-hound lean figure, with a ruined yellow cherub face, in a gray and black glen plaid suit standing near the window of a crowded chicken shack punching the cash register. A woman in the window was tonging golden brown chicken parts from large deepfryers as a bevy of uniformed waitresses served diners at a dozen tables along the wall.

Folks said, "Speedy, pull over and park. I think I saw one of the old gang in that chicken joint. Precious Jimmy, a shill buddy from the old carny days with Blue Howard's flat joints."

Speedy said, "Thank you, that whiskey is got me ready to destroy some cluck," as he pulled the

Eldorado into the curb.

They walked back down the sidewalk teeming with laughing couples and singles peacocking in their Saturday night finery. *Precious Jimmy's Creole Chicken* flashed in orange neon above the door they entered.

Precious exploded at the sight of Folks. "White Folks! My Man!" He scooted from behind the cash register and grabbed Folks in an affectionate bear hug. He led the way to a back room equipped with a sofa, table and chairs surrounded by cartons of store supplies.

Folks said, "You sonuvagun, it's good to see you. Precious, meet Speedy, my partner."

Speedy shook his hand.

Folks said, "Precious, you still a star nine ball player and top craps mechanic?"

They sat on the sofa.

Precious said, "I'm still nine ball champ. I was tops with craps until I played Tango last year and blew this joint to him. You gonna get down in the Windy, Folks?"

"Maybe we will, but not the short con in the streets. I'm itching to rope a hot mark for the long con. White, black or polka dot."

Precious went to a cabinet in the corner. "I've got vodka, gin and Scotch."

"We've been drinking Scotch."

Precious brought back a fifth of Black and White with glasses. He placed bottle and glasses on the table.

Speedy said, "Precious, I'd go for some chicken,

167

dark meat."

Precious said, "I'll get a platter, on the house. What part do you go for, Folks?"

"Dark, Precious, with cole slaw."

Precious went to the curtain separating the rooms and called a waitress to give the order, then came back to sit on the sofa and pour himself a drink from the bottle on the table.

He lit a cigarette, exhaled and said, with hazel eyes ashine, "Say, Speedy, how's your cube game?"

Speedy grinned. "I can trim working marks on payday if I had to. Why, Precious?"

"Don't get me wrong, but Joe Brice . . . uh, Tango and me, were hustlers locking asses to win anyway we could." Precious sighed. "He was just a better craps man, a better cheat. Still, it would thrill me to see somebody kick his ass with the craps, or with any kind of grift, the arrogant, greedy sonuvabitch! I . . . ."

The waitress came through the curtain with a large tray of aromatic chicken and side dishes. She placed it on the table before them and poured two glasses of water from a pitcher. Speedy stuffed a five dollar bill in the front pocket of her tight pink uniform that looked painted on her curves. She smiled and wiggled away through the curtain.

Precious said, "Excuse me a moment." He went into the restaurant.

Speedy and Folks smacked their lips as they attacked the mound of golden chicken.

Speedy said, "Damn! This is good. Best commercial bird I've ever had!"

Folks agreed. "It's fantastic! Franchise this am-
brosia, and the Colonel and the others would have
blues in the night with corporate toothache."

Precious returned as they were smoking cigarettes
and sipping Scotch.

Folks said, "Precious, the chicken is a wipe-
out. What a recipe!"

"Yeah, it's great. My mama's. She died two
months ago, at seventy five. I can't shake the idea
that it was my blowing of our business that nudged
her into the grave. She suffered bad to see me flunky-
ing here as the manager for two bills a week."

Folks said, "You said that Brice was greedy. How
greedy?"

"Well, if you had come to town from Memphis,
scuffling, two years ago and copped the biggest
numbers bank on the southside, this restaurant
that nets two grand a week, silent partner in several
bars, a secret owner of a stable of fighters, would
you be greedy enough to deal dope and risk the
joint?"

Folks said, "He's got the disease! Like a hog
named Paul, he wants it all."

Speedy said, "How the hell did Tango cop all
those goodies in just two years?"

Precious answered, "With the dice at first. I
mean the square dice! The slick bastard can shake
'em and roll 'em across the string and throw anything from two to twelve whenever he wants to.
He beat Sweet Dog out of the numbers bank and
did a black Mafia bit with a gang of gorillas imported from Memphis to cop the rest of his empire.

He's big and treacherous!"

Folks said, "It's interesting about his secret control of a stable of fighters. I'd guess a hog like that would set-up to bet the ones that dived."

"That's Tango's angle."

Speedy said, "Cute moniker, how'd he get it?"

"He was just a club fighter, a chicken shit heavyweight spoiler down south twenty years ago . . . a clutcher and a dancer in the ring."

Folks said, "How do you stand with Tango, Precious? You know, does he really trust you after trimming you?"

Precious grinned. "Yeah, enough so I can burn him for thirty, forty dollars a week. I'm living in his house. I'm good at figures and straight business stuff my mama taught me. Tango is not smart, just slick. He's a rank, loud mouth gorilla. I'd split, take my cue stick on the road with a few grand."

Folks said, "How much liquid draw-it-out-of-bank green would you say Tango is got."

"He's got two hundred grand if he's got a nickel in a safe at home. Why, you think you've got an angle to take him off?"

"I'm just kicking around an angle. Maybe Speedy and I can string it together. If so, you'll get ten percent of the score we take from Tango."

"Folks, you got an angle already. I can tell. You're gonna play for him!"

Folks stood and smiled. "It all depends on you at this point to start the tumblers clicking right. Precious, we need you to bait and hook the mark. We better split before he walks in on us with our heads together. Let's meet somewhere tomorrow."

Precious said, "We can talk now. Tango is in Memphis at his old man's funeral."

Folks sat. "Maybe we can cheer him up when he gets back with a mind-blowing offer to buy the recipe and the right to franchise this chicken shack and the *Precious Jimmy's Creole Chicken* title."

Puzzled doubt creased Precious' face. "Folks, I know you're cinch dynamite with the con, but that sounds like a shaky way to the bread."

Folks grinned. "Precious, do you believe your mama's chicken is delicious enough to franchise across the country?"

"I know damn well it is."

"Well, Tango knows it from the two grand a week he's taking out of the joint free and clear."

Precious dubiously shook his head. "Folks, I can't get the connection to a hunk of Tango's two hundred grand."

"Don't worry about it now. Speedy and I will worry about the connection details. Say, does Tango have a special fighter in his stable? You know, that he's pushing and grooming toward a title?"

"Yeah, a young heavyweight from Memphis. Black Samson, a helluva prospect!"

Precious stared with mouth agape as Speedy leapt to his feet, embraced Folks, kissed his cheek. "It's sweet! Bait the mark with the franchise offer then switch him and play him against the old fight con, up-dated. It fits Tango like a pigskin glove, no pun intended."

Folks said, "When does Tango get back to

Chicago?"

Precious answered, "In the next several days."

"Mellow! Precious, when he gets back tell him how a black Mister Carl Davis ate your chicken and flipped over it. Mister Davis returned two nights later with his white boss, me, a Mister ah . . . let's see, I'll give you that name later to fit a real Loop businessman. The chicken freaked me out. Then lay the golden hook line on Tango. I am president of a conglomerate company involved in the food and services franchise industries. We'll have an answering service contact and business cards for you tomorrow, Precious."

Speedy said, "Precious, it's very important to mention that my white boss was here with me on my second visit. Maybe one of those waitresses out there is a spy for Tango or just a flap jaw who might crack that a white guy was back here tonight with you."

Folks said, "Where do Tango's fighters train? I'd like to gander Samson in the gym."

"Tango's set up a private gym in the rear of his house. Full scale ring, the whole works."

Speedy exclaimed, "Folks, this is so sweet I can't believe it!"

"Precious, any chance we can see that gym alone before Tango gets back?"

"Sure, tonight after I close the joint." Precious glanced at his wristwatch. "It's eleven-thirty. Come back at two-fifteen and follow me home. It's just fifteen minutes from here."

Folks said, "We'll be back."

172

Precious put his arm around Folks' shoulder. "Folks, I love you like a brother. Maybe you shouldn't play for Tango. He'll hurt you bad if he tips during the play."

"Precious, he won't tip to our airtight play. Tonight the three of us will rehearse the 'hook' to the bone."

They shook hands with Precious and went to the Eldorado. Speedy pulled it into traffic, then groaned. "Well, there goes my chance to grease my jones unless I can long-shot and shoot some fox down in the coffee shop at our hotel."

Folks laughed. "You're right, partner. The joints are out for us tonight. We can't expose ourselves together at all. In fact, it would be wise the day that Tango gobbles the bait that I split to a class hotel suite in the Loop."

Speedy laughed. "Boss, sir, that move will sho 'nuff be convenient to our Loop franchise office set-up."

They laughed.

Then Speedy said, "Precious is bright, but I wonder if he can take the cues and handle all the crossfire lines of the 'hook' with on-the-money-split-second-timing."

"He can handle it. I got no doubt . . . after we rehearse him."

Speedy pulled the car to a halt at a stoplight as Folks glanced at a couple in an alley. A tall dude was frantically trying, but failing, to block street view of his woman squatting and spewing urine on the alley floor.

Folks remembered, with a shudder, when years before in a drunken helpless tailspin over loss of Camille Costain, the heartless white Goddess, he had been mistaken for white and been violated on Scoville Avenue in Cleveland's black ghetto.

It had been midnight when he found himself at the shabby corner of Thirty-ninth Street and Scoville Avenue. It was central headquarters for dope peddlers and whores. He'd never know why he'd been stupid enough to park and stumble into a funky bar on the corner, crowded with profane whores and drunken tricks. He took a stool and a double shot in a corner near the back door.

The heat in the crowded room was terrific. He couldn't take off his overcoat because of the roll of dough stashed in the lining, afraid the coat might get away from him. He stood up and was bending his elbow to drain his glass when a toothless old black whore reeled into him. Runny sores covered her face.

He staggered back and said, "Goddamn, watch it, Grandmaw!"

She grinned up at him vacantly, wiped the snotty sleeve of her mangy rabbit fur coat across her drippy flat nose and simpered, "Whitey, I got the hottest pussy on this corner. C'mon and have some fun. You can go three-way for a tray. C'mon, Whitey, and spend something with Louise."

He backed up to the wall from her stinking breath and the clouds of crotch rot.

She clutched the front of his shirt and shouted, "Why don't you spend a chicken-shit tray with

174

Louise?"

He knocked her hand away with his elbow, but she grabbed and twisted her fingers into his shirt front again. He was angry and dizzy. He had to escape the bedlam of the spinning room.

He blurted, "Louise, you're a joke. You're old and funky and ugly. You should have retired fifty years ago. Get your goddamn hand off me!"

She jerked her hand away and glared at him as he stumbled out the back door. The snowy ground was revolving like a giant record on a wobbly turntable. He threw his hands out as the frightful whiteness catapulted up toward him.

He stirred. He felt something crawling, patting and moving across his clothes. He opened his dazed eyes. A dark crouching shape was silhouetted against the star-infested sky. He tried to move away from the busy shadow with the familiar rotten stink. But his muscles were paralyzed.

Then the shape moved out of sight behind him. Suddenly the sky was blotted out, and he seemed to be trapped in a pitch black tent. And the familiar stink was overpowering. He heard a cackling giggle and a hot pungent rain splattered his face and scalded his eyes. He lay there groaning and twisting his head from side to side in the stinking blackness.

He felt a feathery sweep of the tent across his face as it slid away to bare the cold blue stars again. He lay there gasping and sucking in the wonderful wintry air, feeling his muscles quivering back to life. He was rising on his elbows when a horde of shadows came through the back door and stood in a silent circle around him. They fumbled at their flies.

He jerked up and sat there screaming at them, as he had screamed at the black racists who had chased him with knives on Chicago's Forty-third Street when he was a boy. "I'm a nigger! I'm a nigger!"

The cruel bastards just laughed and started kicking him. He wrapped his arms around his face against the crushing barrage of feet ripping into him from head to ankles. He crashed on his side and faintly heard the steady patter of terrible rain against his numbness.

Then the laughter, the numbness and the patter of the reeky rain were lost in a yawning black pit of nothingness.

Now, he heard Speedy say, "Well, pally, we're home."

Folks was grateful for the fresh air of reality as he got out of the car and followed Speedy into their hotel. In the lobby, Speedy craned his neck to ogle a gaggle of young foxes seated at the counter in the coffee shop. He took several steps toward the chattering sexpots, halted and got into the elevator with Folks.

He sighed. "I can't really get in a pussy mood, pally, with a mark on the turn with two hundred grand in a home damper."

Folks said, "What saves you, partner, is you're just a part-time trick."

Speedy gave him a jab in the arm as the elevator took flight.

15

TWO DAYS LATER on Monday, Precious called Speedy's answering service from Tango's house with a message for Mister Carl Davis to call Tango at home. Speedy did and made a Wednesday afternoon appointment with Tango at his house.

Wednesday noon, Folks and Speedy sat in the swank Loop hotel suite that Folks had checked into that morning as Mister Steven Hoffman. Vicksburg Kid and Tear Off Thomas, Harlem brute-built young grifter and former pro knockout artist handicapped by a fragile jaw, checked into a suite down the hall. At one-twenty, Speedy left the suite in chauffeur's uniform for a rented limo to keep his two o'clock appointment with Tango.

Precious winked as he said, "Good afternoon,

Mister Davis," and let him into the livng room of the sprawling white stucco house crammed with expensive modern furniture.

Speedy sat on a twenty foot red silk sofa. There was the raucous sound of a craps game from the rear of the house.

Precious whispered, "The hog is rooting the loot from some sucker hustlers from Milwaukee. I'll get him," as he left the room through an archway.

Speedy leapt to his feet, with chauffeur's cap in hand, stooped a bit, knees dipped a fraction in perfect role play of the genuflective servant. Tango's six-four brawny frame filled the archway as he entered the room with Precious. He had the malevolent black face of a Sonny Liston and a ninety percent gold-toothed smile as he cat-walked red lizard shoes and green plaid suit across the carpet to Speedy.

Precious said, "Mister Brice, Mister Davis."

Tango said, "Brother Davis, it's beautiful to meet you," as he seized Speedy's hand in a mammoth paw and pumped it.

Speedy said, "Sure is a pleasure for me too, Mister Brice," as the trio sat down on the sofa.

Tango leaned close to Speedy and studied his face for a long moment. "I like you, brother, you look like good people."

Speedy averted his eyes in the shy fashion of a coquette. "Thank you, sir."

Tango's face registered terminal pain. "Brother, don't call me nothing but Tango."

"Mist . . . uh, Tango, thank you. You can call

me Carl if you want."

Tango turned and spanked Precious' thigh. "Get Carl a taste while we rap 'bout chicken and peckerwoods."

Speedy said, "Thank you, but I don't drink since I got my ulcer operation last year."

"Brother, I wanted to see you up front before I rapped any business with your boss. Gimme a run-down on Hoffman."

Speedy said, "I brought him to eat your chicken and he wants the world to enjoy it and get richer than he is." Speedy enjoyed an interior chuckle as he added, " . . . which is the name of the game for white folks."

Tango said, "Brother, don't feed me no a-b-c's! I mean rundown your boss' character, like his track record. Is the peckerwood honest?"

"Sure, he's white business man honest, as honest as the contract you sign. When you get it, take it unsigned to a lawyer who is expert in contracts. You got one?"

"He's out of town, but he's the best mouth-piece fixer in Chi. He's handled my contracts with fighters."

Precious said, "Tango, Hawkins is basically a criminal lip. He'd be in trouble with a corporation contract."

Speedy said, "Tango, you can take the contract and a couple of hundred dollars to a contract specialist. All you need now is the contract."

Tango banged Speedy's shoulder. "You're a beautiful brother, in my corner like a true blue nigger oughtta be. I'm gonna stick him up for a hundred grand before I Hancock a fucking contract. How about that?"

Speedy shook his head emphatically. "Brother Tango, we gonna lose our new friendship, and my respect for you, if you don't demand a million dollars!"

Tango's eyes sparkled excitement. "A million dollars?"

"Why not, brother? Here's a secret. One of his father's subsidiary companies gave the Colonel a million. Your chicken makes his garbage by comparison. You know that's the truth."

Speedy slipped on a bitter mask of seriousness as he prepared to spin the first segment of the con tale. "I'm an honest man, on the square with honest men. I'm no traitor to my boss. Let me share something personal with you brothers, my reasons why, beyond that we're black brothers, that I want to see you get a good white folks deal against my boss' business interests. Brothers, listen to the truth.

"I been flun . . . uh, working for the Hoffman family since Steven Hoffman, Junior was a snot-nosed kid. Like the mammies in slave days, I know them and a lot of their secrets. I'll say it! Hoffman, Senior treated me like I was white before his health failed seven years ago and he let Junior pretend that he's in control. I was, more than anything else, the old man's companion and friend.

"Now, I'm the son's go-for. He misused a close friend of mine and I'll never forgive him! So, brother, be convinced I'm on your side all the way.

180

Demand a million!"

Tango seized Speedy in a bear hug, leapt to his feet. "Right on, brother! I'll settle for nothing but a mil," he exclaimed as he excitedly paced the carpet. Then he said to Precious, with a beatific smile, "Ain't Brother Carl something else?"

Precious answered, "He's the greatest! If black people had more like him, we coud give greedy whitey's pocketbook a black eye!"

Tango flopped down on the sofa, twanging with excitement, between Speedy and Precious. He said, "When do I see your boss?"

Speedy glanced at his wristwatch. "Why not this afternoon? He's anxious and available until five. Should I call and make an appointment?"

"Great!" and he lifted the phone from the coffee table onto Speedy's lap.

Speedy dialed the fake office and Folks' receptionist answered. "Carl Davis for Mister Hoffman, Junior, please."

The mark leaned his ear close to the receiver.

Folks' voice came on the line. "Yes, Carl."

Speedy pushed the back of the receiver against Tango's ear. "I'm at Mister Brice's home. He's available for a conference with you this afternoon."

"Splendid, Carl. Put him on."

Speedy gave Tango the receiver. He said, "I'm Joe Brice, Mister Hoffman, the owner of the chicken shack."

Folks said, "It's a pleasure to meet you. I would be delighted to see you this afternoon. Would four-thirty be convenient for you? Please bring your restaurant ownership documents."

Tango's voice shook with excitement. "Why yes, I'll be there."

"See you then, Mister Brice."

Tango cradled the phone and replaced it on the table. He glanced at his wristwatch and stood.

"Carl, it's just three-thirty. C'mon, I'll let you dig my place," he said as he walked toward the archway followed by Precious and Speedy.

Tango unlocked a door, went in, came back stuffing an envelope into his coat pocket. "Don't want to forget the restaurant papers," he said as he locked the door and moved down the hallway.

Tango stopped at the doorway of a room just beyond the archway. Three sharply dressed middle-aged black men stood around a felt-covered table shooting craps.

Tango said, "Friends, I'll be back to the fun in a couple of hours."

The gamblers nodded with loser scowls.

Speedy oohed and ahhed as Tango showed him through the two story, flashily-furnished five bed-room house. At the rear of the house, Tango paused at the open door of a rec room. Speedy stared at a half dozen of the toughest looking hoods in his memory watching a pair of their group shooting pool. They all raised their eyes and stared coldly at Speedy.

Tango went to one of the pool shooters and whispered into his ear, as Precious whispered, from the side of his mouth to Speedy, "The Tango Mob!"

182

Tango turned and rejoined them, leading the... into the back yard toward a large bungalow. Speedy heard the whump of boxing gloves and the staccato whap of a light punching bag used to sharpen boxer timing. They entered the gym and were enveloped in a pungent smog of resin and sweat.

Eight of Tango's fighters, in trunks, from light-weights to a pair of heavies, were punching the light and heavy bags. Others shadow boxed. An old ox-shouldered ex-pug, cauliflowered and tar black, refereed two sweat-shiny black heavies in head-gear, sparring violently, punching and grunting, in the pro size ring in the center of the room. Speedy followed Tango and Precious to a row of seats at ringside. Samson's trunks bore his name.

As they sat down, Tango chortled, "You seeing young black Samson, the next world heavyweight champion, in action."

For several minutes Speedy sat between them gazing raptly up at tawny black Samson deliver-ing his wizard repertoire of combinations to the face and body of the older pug until a Samson right cross smashed scarlet from his spar mate's nose and the brute-faced referee called time.

Speedy glazed his eyes, muttered incoherently as he rocked and wrung his hands. Precious watched, with smug amusement, as Speedy's performance affected Tango with wide-eyed, absolute flabber-gast, all according to game plan. Tango's jaw dropped slack, mesmerized as he watched Speedy cry out and leap into the ring, seizing Samson in a bear hug.

The astonished giant stared down at Tango in complete bewilderment as Speedy blubbered, "You're another miracle, son! God bless and keep your talents!" Speedy released him suddenly and with a far away look, parted the ropes and left the ring. He muttered, "My friends, let's get to our appointment," as he passed Precious and Tango.

He walked trance-like through the house and out the front door to the limousine, unlocked it and extended the keys to Precious.

"Please drive, brother. I'm not in shape."

Precious said, "Sure, Carl." Then he took Folks' business card from his shirt pocket, glanced at it and pulled the limo away.

There was a thunderous silence in the car until Precious tooled the limo onto the Outer Drive for the Loop. "Brother Carl, what . . . ah, excuse me, but what happened back there in the gym?" Precious asked gently.

Speedy stared ahead as he mumbled, "Please Jimmy, forget it, will you?"

Tango stared curiously at Speedy's profile as he patted Speedy's knee. "Brother, you good peoples. We like you. Trust us and maybe you can unload some of the burden that's bugging you. Okay?"

Speedy's face was agonized, his voice strident. "Damn it, brothers, don't quiz me no more about it. Anyway, it's your fault, Tango, that you showed me Samson!"

Tango said, "I sure didn't mean to put the hurt to you, brother, after you tipped me how to cop a mil and protect myself 'gainst the peckerwood.

184

I'm sorry."

A moment later Speedy mumbled in a whisper, "And I'm sorry I said what I did. I feel guilty I didn't tip you all the way."

Tango said, "What!?"

"Their contract is going to take your chicken shack and you out of the Precious Jimmy Creole Chicken business."

Tango exclaimed, "I don't give a fuck! Not if I get a million dollars, brother. I'll lay you odds the Colonel didn't give a fuck!"

Speedy smiled. "But Tango, if they don't get your joint, it could make you another million or so."

Tango snorted. "I'm almost fifty years old. Ain't no guarantee I'm gonna live so I can take two grand a week for ten years outta that joint. 'Sides, it's a assache even with Precious managing. Brother, I don't need no chicken with a million dollars!"

"But they'll spend millions to advertise on t.v., radio, newspapers. They'll make that chicken a household word. We could triple, even quadruple two grand a week if we got addenda to their contract giving us the exclusive right to sell Precious Jimmy Chicken on the southside."

Tango exclaimed, "We!?"

"I'm an old man, brother. My bosses will wake up, down the line, that only I could have tipped you how to demand the addenda, tipped you to how anxious my boss and his father are to franchise your chicken. Brother, isn't it fair that I be your partner in the restaurant after I get fired for tipping you how to keep it? We don't need our agreement on paper since we black brothers, do we? Tango, I knew I could trust you when I met you. You know you can trust me. Just your handshake will satisfy me."

Tango extended his hand. "It's fair! You got a deal, beautiful brother. Run it down to me."

They shook hands passionately.

Speedy said, "Does Jimmy have any piece of the restaurant?"

Tango darted a guilty look at Precious' impassive face behind the wheel. "No, brother, I . . . uh, bought him out a hundred percent. Why?"

Speedy said softly, "We can't be greedy can we? It wouldn't be fair to leave a fine manager and person like Jimmy out in the cold. I say let's share a third of the restaurant with him. If it's all right with you, Tango."

Tango said, "Great! That's great. That's a deal, too."

Speedy extended his hand and shook Tango's flaccid duke. "Okay, then here's the rundown from a to z. Remember, Tango, you're not going to get a million dollar offer up front. You have to demand a million. Get up and walk out if they back up on your mil demand and your demands to keep the restaurant and the exclusive right to sell our chicken on the southside. You got to have the balls to split if . . . ."

Tango cut him off. "Look Carl, suppose I blow the deal pressing the peckerwoods on them addenda?"

Precious said, "Tango, we on the outside. The brother is on the inside. The brother knows. You got to trust the brother and play your hand like he runs it down."

Speedy added, "Tango, you can't blow the deal. The worst you can do is postpone it if you have to split today. They'll come back to you on your terms in a week or so. Be strong and patient, brother, and get it all!"

Tango sighed. "I'll play it strong Jones with those peckerwoods, right down the line!"

Precious said, "We're almost there and it's get-down time, Tango," as he moved the limo through the raucous honk of Loop traffic.

At the end of the block, Precious pulled into the subterranean garage of a skyscraper office building. An attendant gave Precious a ticket at the entrance, then Precious cruised the limo through the cool murk to a parking space. He shut off the engine, started to get out.

Speedy said, "Easy, Jimmy," as he glanced at his wristwatch.

Tango said, "That clock on the wall over there says we're four minutes late."

"We're not late enough. Let 'em stew."

Speedy extended his cigarette pack, flicked flame to their cigarettes, lit his own. He took a long draw, exhaled it against the windshield.

Precious said, "Carl, you sure got a hard-on for your boss. Hoorah for me and Tango."

Speedy sighed and mused the con switch. "Yeah, I guess you're right, Precious. And I don't like feeling a need for revenge against Junior Hoffman. He's not all bad, but he's more bad than good. Rotten! It hurts me to betray him, to betray any man. I never have before in my long life, but he deserves it! Brothers, seeing young Samson all aglow with youth and great promise in the ring broke me up. You see, Junior is to blame for prostituting, ruining the youth, my dreams for a protege I love like a blood brother.

"I discovered Upshaw in a Harlem gym six years ago. As a former club fighter and trainer, I knew instantly he was a natural gem with the ballet moves of Sugar Ray and the stamina, heart and punch of Marciano. Well, I didn't have the long bread it would take to develop him properly. You know, cut him loose from his bouncer gig in a bucket-of-blood bar that kept the grits and greens flowing for his ma and pa and ten younger brothers and sisters.

"Well, to make a short story shorter, I turned Upshaw over to a manager's contract with Hoffman. In six months I buffed off Upshaw's rough edges and created a dynamite fighting machine. Right away, Hoffman took us on a tour of Europe, Berlin, Rome and Paris, fighting and beating the best. I was puzzled at first why Hoffman insisted that Upshaw fight under aliases. I pleaded with him to let Upshaw's name and talent burst out on the world so he could become a legit heavyweight contender with ranking and a shot at the world crown.

"Brothers, maybe you've guessed why Hoffman

wanted Upshaw under the barrel of obscurity. He was fleecing rich sportsmen out of a fortune by betting ringer Upshaw could beat their favorite boxers, usually at bandit odds. Hoffman didn't share a nickel of that fortune with Upshaw or me. The bouts were held in small clubs. The purses were miserly and Upshaw's youth and dreams were drained away by those six years in Europe.

"A specialist, in Berlin, told me last year to retire Upshaw after he was knocked out in the last of three boys in three days. The doctor said Upshaw has an inoperable clot on the brain, and that a hard punch to the head could kill him. I've kept that a secret from Hoffman because I know he'd dump Upshaw like a broken toy. Now you know, brothers, why Junior is the only human in this world that I hate!"

Precious said, "Brother, I hate that snake too, just off what you told us."

Tango said breathlessly, "Carl, you gotta take me to Europe and let me bankroll that action when Upshaw dives."

"Wish you could, Tango. Now, let's get up to Hoffman's office and do the contract number."

They got out of the machine and Tango embraced Speedy. "Carl, you're a beautiful brother and I love ya!"

As they walked away, Speedy glanced at his watch, synched with the Vicksburg Kid's, who waited. They took an elevator to the fifth floor.

The Kid, skillfully aged to an octogenarian complete with elegant black apparel, hearing aid and heavy gold-headed cane, peeped around a corner at them as they left the elevator and came down the corridor. He limped through a door stenciled *Steven Hoffman And Associates, International Franchise, Inc.*

Kid went to the desk of the receptionist and said, "Dear young lady, would you be so kind as to tell me whether the investment counselors Peake And Associates have an office on this floor? I don't see well and I'm tuckered out."

She smiled. "That firm is on the floor above, the sixth."

"Thank you, dearie."

He turned away, paused to light a cigarette at the frosted glass door, then stepped out into the corridor at the instant that he saw the shadows of Speedy and the others turn the corner. They nearly collided.

Tango glanced at the *Hoffman* stencil on the office door at the moment that Speedy exclaimed, "Mister Hoffman, sir, what a surprise!"

Kid embraced Speedy. "Carl, it's good to see you." Kid's eyes twinkled mischievously through fake bifocal windows. "I dare say Steven was also surprised when I flew in last night to reorganize things a bit. I presume you and these gentlemen have business with him?"

Speedy said, "Why yes, we do have an appointment. Traffic made us late. These gentlemen, Joe Brice and Jimmy Allen, are the Precious Jimmy Chicken people. I hope Steven hasn't gone."

Kid said, "Glad to meet you, gentlemen," as

190

he shook hands with Precious and Tango. "I can assure you, Carl, that Steven is waiting. He froze me a sample of that chicken." Kid bunched fingertips against his pursed lips. "Ah, gentlemen! Even reheated from the freezer, your chicken was a luscious benediction to my taste buds."

Tango and Precious chorused, "Thank you, Mister Hoffman!"

Speedy took a step to lead them toward the door of the legitimate Hoffman firm.

Kid winked his eye at Precious and Tango and chuckled, "Carl, another surprise. I have come out of retirement!"

Speedy turned with a surprised face. "What!?"

Kid grinned. "I told you time and again, my retirement wasn't permanent. I've taken over my old desk. Come with me to Steven's office down the corridor."

They followed him as he led the way.

Kid said, "Steven's new responsibilities are contracts and market research."

The group approached a door stenciled *Global Market Research, Inc.* Kid stepped aside and swung open the door. Then they all stepped into a lavish reception room, muraled and airy beige-carpeted. A cute blonde receptionist smiled at them from behind a curved desk.

Kid said, "Carol, Mister Brice is here to see Steven."

16

THEY SAT IN CHAIRS in Folks' opulent office watching Tango squinting and frowning as he laboriously read the last of the four page contract. He passed it to Precious, who started to read it. Tango leaned toward Folks, who sat bland-faced, Brooks Brothers-draped, behind his gleaming mahogany desk with prop family photographs of a ravishing blonde wife and tow-headed young children on the desk top.

Tango said, "I can't sign these papers, Mister Hoffman, for two hundred and fifty thousand dollars."

Folks smiled. "Mister Brice, it's a standard franchise contract with a . . . uh, tentative offer figure. How much do you want?"

Tango jutted out his rocky jaw. "I want a million!"

Folks winced. "A million dollars, Mister Brice?"

"You heard me."

"How about a half million?"

Tango said, "You gonna take my chicken and make enough money to barbecue a wet elephant. I want a million!"

Folks turned to Kid, seated beside him. "What do you think, Dad?"

Kid's face creased in apparent concentrated thought. After a long moment he shrugged. "A half million, a million, what's the difference when you consider it's just a ledger entry for the accountants and our tax people to square up."

Folks picked up an intercom to summon his secretary, a junoesque brunette, from an adjoining office.

"Ann, please take this contract and the copy that Mister Allen has and change the amount to one million dollars."

Shortly she returned and placed the papers on the desk before she went back into her office.

Folks said, "It's a pleasure to do business with you, Mister Brice," as he shoved the copy of the contract and a pen across the desk top toward Tango.

Tango squared up his heavy shoulders, crossed his steel cable legs, picked a mote of lint from his green suit. He stared unhappily at the contract with narrowed maroon eyes. Then he resolutely shook his glittery processed buffalo head. "Mister

Hoffman, you ain't got nothing there yet for me to Hancock."

Folks and Kid exchanged puzzled and distressed looks.

Tango shot a look at Speedy, beaming proudly, and said, "You gonna have to call that girl back and let her tack on a pair of addenda in that contract. I got to keep my chicken shack and I gotta be the only one on the southside selling Precious Chicken."

Folks shoved himself back from the desk with maximal aggravation on his face. "Ridiculous! I can't do it! Mister Brice, a deal like that is unprecedented!"

Tango started to rise, faltered, shot an agonized look at Speedy. Speedy hardened his eyes, nodded almost imperceptibly to prod Tango to hang tough and split.

Tango tightened his jaw, hauled himself out of the chair, swallowed and said stoutly, "Since you can't do it, Mister Hoffman, I'm walking. I ain't on welfare." He turned and walked toward the door, followed by Precious.

The players let them go through the door, waited long moments before Folks said, "All right, Speedy, reel him back in."

Speedy went after them, spotted them at the elevator and whistled as they were stepping into it. "C'mon back, brothers! We've won!"

The corridor resounded as they spanked palms and embraced one another. Tango hugged Speedy's waist and lifted him into the air as passersby gawked.

"Shit, brother, you got to be the greatest nigger

there ever was. I love ya!''

Speedy said, "Now, brother, remember you don't sign the contract until I can dig us up a contract expert. Pick up the contract and split again."

Tango said, "Brother Genuis, I can dig it. I'm letting you call the shots!''

They entered, went into Folks' office. Kid was sitting in Folks' leather throne behind the desk, smiling charmingly. Folks sat, morosely, in Kid's chair.

Kid said, "Congratulations, Mister Brice. I have decided to meet your demands. Ann is inserting the addenda you requested. Please relax and have a seat. You're dealing with me now."

They seated themselves. Ann brought back the contracts, placed pen, and the copy of the contract on the desk top before Tango, smiled and departed.

Kid said, "Mister Brice, for a layman, you're an absolute whiz at getting your way in a business transaction," as he darted a hooded, suspicious look at Speedy.

Tango stood, snatched the contract off the desk top and grinned. "I got mother wit, Mister Hoffman. I'll call you and sign after a lawyer fine-tooths these papers."

"Of course, Mister Brice, that's your privilege." Kid stood and leaned across the desk to pump Tango's hand.

Then Folks came to shake Tango's hand. He said, Mister Brice, your demands shook me up a bit. I'm sorry, I hope there are no hard feelings."

Tango banged Folks' shoulder. "Everything is mellow, Mister Hoffman. See ya." Tango turned away for the door, followed by Precious and Speedy.

Folks said, "Carl, I'd like you to drop me off at the gym before you take Mister Brice and Mister Allen home. I want to check up on Upshaw's condition."

Speedy said, "Why not, boss?"

Kid said sternly, "Steven, I certainly hope that you stay away from that gambling den in that building where the gym is located. Gamblers are neurotics, prone to pain and disgrace. Protect our name as your dear departed mother would wish."

"Dad, I haven't taken a bet since that raid in college. I share your views about gamblers."

"That's my boy!"

As Folks started to leave the office with the others, Kid said pleasantly, "Hope to see you soon, Mister Brice. Oh Steven, may I have a brief word with you?"

Folks turned. "Of course, Dad," then said over his shoulder, "Carl, you may take the gentlemen to the car. I'll join you shortly."

Speedy led them to the limousine's front seat cushions. They sat smoking in silence for several moments until Tango said, "Brother Carl, you and Upshaw really are boss squares if you wait to start a nest-egg with that dago in the old country. Brother, your boss is ready now for the killing floor!"

Precious exclaimed, "Tango, I know what you're

thinking. And it's mellow!"

Speedy said, "Me and Upshaw been waiting to do business in Rome because Sergio is the only one with enough bankroll to make Upshaw's . . . ah, loss worthwhile for us. He guarantees us fifty percent of what the boss loses. We trust him, I trust you, so share your thoughts, Tango."

Before Tango could reply, Speedy's eyes caught fire. He snapped his fingers. "Don't tell me, brother! In a week or so you'll have a big bankroll from the franchise deal. Then we can arrange a private bout between Samson and Upshaw. Junior makes reparations, a hundred grand or so when Upshaw loses. You bet Hoffman bread against Junior. Brother Tango, what beautiful thinking you do!"

Tango's Neanderthal face was smug. "Carl, you been playing me cheap. We ain't gotta wait for that deal to intercourse Junior outta the first bundle."

"What *first* bundle, brother?"

"You heard me. Why shit, after the franchise deal goes down, Junior's nose will be wide open for a re-match. That is, if Samson and Upshaw do a secret rehearsal before they have the first bout."

Speedy leaned across Precious from behind the wheel and pumped Tango's hand. "Brother, it's brilliant!" But even as his praise echoed, Speedy frowned. He slumped behind the wheel, apparently crestfallen. "There's too much risk. After losing that first bundle, suppose Junior gets the idea that we rigged the bout to cheat him. He'll get salty and maybe cancel the franchise deal."

Tango said, "That square-ass peckerwood can't

wake up if our fighters rehearse. 'Sides, his old man is handling my deal, and 'sides that, you heard how his old man feels about gambling. Junior is tee-rolled!"

Speedy's brows hedge-rowed in thought before he said, "What's your opinion, Precious?"

Precious answered, "Tango is right. Junior is in a box."

Speedy nodded toward Folks stepping from the elevator into the garage. "All right Tango, me and Upshaw are in, if you can prod Junior into a bout. You take over, brother."

Speedy started the car and eased it abreast of Folks, then leapt out to open the rear car door for Folks. Speedy shut the door behind him, went behind the wheel and drove them into the late afternoon traffic.

Twenty minutes later, they sat inhaling sweat and resin odors on a row of reclaimed wooden movie seats at a ringside in the spacious two ring gym. It was resonating with *grunt*, *smash* and *whish* sounds of two dozen black and white pro boxers honing their skills, jumping rope and banging punching bags.

The Folks' group's eyes were riveted to the gargantuan Upshaw, in tights and training helmet. His hawk face blossomed sweat as his sleek muscles undulated beneath his inky skin. He thumped and peppered his bullish Mexican spar mate with ferocious jabs and hooks to the face and body as he feinted, danced and sidestepped with superstar matador finesse.

198

In a clinch, Upshaw's eye flicked across ringside and snared Speedy's twitch of right eyebrow signal. The white haired mulatto referee stepped in and separated them. Upshaw rammed a wicked left hook into his opponent's solar plexus, followed by a crunching right cross to the chin that flew his mouthpiece through the air like a mini Frisbee. The Mexican shook, for a moment, like a cerebral palsy victim before he crashed backward to the canvas and lay motionless in kayo slumber.

Handlers leapt into the ring with smelling salts to revive the boxer, who left the ring on rubbery legs. Harlem grifter Tear Off Thomas, alias Upshaw, climbed from the ring. Folks stood and blotted off his sweat with a Turkish towel. He flung a terrycloth robe across Upshaw's shoulders and gave him a bottle of Gator Ade as Upshaw sprawled himself on the row of seats between Tango and Folks.

Folks said, "Good boy, Upshaw! I'm proud of you. Your timing is exquisite and your combinations are cooking."

"Thank you, Mister Hoffman. Does that mean you'll try to get me a fight soon here in the States, maybe with a ranked contender?"

Folks removed his gloves and patted his shoulder. "I've thought about it, Upshaw. You deserve and are qualified for a shot like that. However, there isn't time to arrange an important match like that. Two months from today we fly to the Continent to fight the number one contender for the European title. I called Rome this morning to make the arrangements."

Upshaw slumped his shoulders, stared disconsolately at the floor.

Folks jabbed his shoulder. "Cheer up for me, Upshaw, and perhaps I can arrange to get you on the card next month here in the stadium in the main event."

Then he sighed. "That is, if the matchmaker can dig up an adequate opponent on such short notice. It'll be virtually impossible for any unranked heavy in America to stand against your attack for more than two rounds. I'd like to insure you some tune-up action and the buffs a run for the price of their tickets."

Tango snickered.

Folks leaned across Upshaw. "Why do my remarks about my fighter amuse you, Mister Brice?"

Tango grinned and jogged a manicured index finger down the razor crease in his trousers. "'Cause you jiving yourself, Mister Hoffman!"

"Jiving myself, Mister Brice?" Folks asked with rising heat.

Tango smirked. "Yeah! You remind me of them kooky jokers that seen the moon in a pool of water and tried to cop it with a rake. Mister Hoffman, you ain't got to waste no time moon raking to find a heavyweight to sweat Upshaw. I got one that will pop sweat and fire outta Upshaw's old ass. I got one that can beat Upshaw!"

Folks said, "This marvel of yours, anyone anybody has ever heard of?"

"Everybody is gonna hear about young Samson,

the champ in a couple years."

Folks frowned in thought for a long moment, then he laughed. "Samson! He's just a novice with moderate promise. I saw him in a pre-lim at the stadium. Why, he can't be more than twenty years old, raw and unseasoned, fresh out of amateur competition!"

Upshaw glowered and sneered. "Brice, I'll chase any green punk like that back up his mammy's ass. I want Samson, Mister Hoffman!"

Folks tightened his face in fake apprehension as he massaged Upshaw's neck, corded in grifter rage as he stared balefully into Tango's eyes. Upshaw rhythmically sledged his fists against his thighs. His jaw muscles rolled and lumped.

Folks crooned, "Easy now, Upshaw, get hold of yourself. Don't do anything foolish. Remember you fight for money, not for fun. Forget Samson. I can't let you fight pre-lims. That's all a matchmaker would give us with Samson. Now go to the showers."

Upshaw stood, then glared down at Tango before he turned away.

Tango loud-mouthed, "Oh, Mister Hoffman! Thank you! I'm so glad you called off your ugly gorilla before I crapped my pants!"

Upshaw spun back, fearsome face contorted as he lunged for Tango as Tango leapt to his feet in a combat crouch. A small crowd gathered. Speedy jumped between them and led Upshaw away beyond earshot of the ringside.

"Tear Off, that was sweet! Play the gorilla for

the mark until I cut him in as a friend later on," Speedy whispered as he smacked the giant's rump.

Speedy turned and joined the others at ringside.

Tango was saying, "You heard me right, Mister Hoffman. We'll put up a respectable purse for a private bout. The winning fighter takes the pot . . . unless you done changed your opinion about your gorilla being so great."

Folks frowned and procrastinated a response.

Tango goaded, "Well, Mister Hoffman, you eating crow?"

Folks smiled. "We'll fight Samson, Mister Brice. But not in your personal ghetto ring, not with the ill feelings you forced between Upshaw and yourself."

Tango snickered. "You copped out! You know they can't fight in the alley. You afraid to fight Samson, ain't you?"

"Hell no!" Then he stood and walked away.

The trio watched Folks enter a glassed-in cubicle at the far end of the room with *Office* stenciled on its door. Folks smiled charmingly at the cauliflowered owner of the gym, seated behind a blistered desk.

"My name is Jelke, Mister Dolan. As a manager, I want to congratulate you for having a truly fine facility here." Folks shook hands with the battered ancient and seated himself in front of the desk.

The trio, at ringside, watched Folks animatedly chatting with Dolan in the manner of old friends.

Precious said, "I wonder what he's doing in there?"

Speedy offered, "Knowing Junior, I'd bet he's

making arrangements with his old friend Dolan to stage our fight, privately, right here."

Tango said, "You're right! I told you we could trim him!"

Folks came back to join them with a radiant face. The trio stood.

"Well, Mister Brice, it's all set. This gym closes early tomorrow at two p.m. At three, we'll have our bout in private with Mister Dolan as referee. Any questions, Mister Brice?" asked Folks.

Tango said, "I don't like the referee, if he's gonna judge the fight solo."

"Would you still have that objection if we agreed to a fight to the finish? Mister Brice, you can referee since I'm confident Upshaw will knock out your guy early on. Mister Dolan will preside simply to break clinches. Well?"

Tango grinned. "Your way suits me. What kinda purse we gonna put up?"

Folks said, "I'll cover, in cash, any amount of cash you bring to wager, Mister Brice. Carl will pick you and Samson up in the early afternoon tomorrow for a meeting before the bout. Agreed?"

"I sure do. See you tomorrow!"

Folks turned to Speedy. "Carl, I've invited Mister Dolan to cocktails down the street. Please wait and take Upshaw to his hotel."

Folks shook hands with Tango and Precious before he turned away and walked back toward the office. They watched him as he paused to speak briefly with Upshaw, togged out in a noisy maroon ensemble, with his boxer's bag in hand. Speedy led the way to Upshaw as Folks walked away to enter the office.

Speedy said, "Come on, Upshaw, I'll drop you at your hotel before I take these gentlemen to the southside."

Upshaw glared homicide at Tango. "Carl, I ain't riding with this jive-ass nigger. I'm afraid I'll tear his fucking head off and get in trouble with Mister Hoffman! I'll get a cab."

Speedy laughed. "Relax, old buddy. Meet Tango and Precious Jimmy, our friends. They're with us to set up Junior for a big buck killing."

Upshaw's eyes popped wide in complete flabbergast. "Well, I'll be a sonuvabitch!" he exclaimed. "Damn! Brother Tango, you had me fooled."

Upshaw darted a glance toward Folks in the office before he pumped Tango and Precious' hands. They left the building for the parking lot behind the gym.

Speedy drove the Outer Drive to the southside where, minutes later, he, Upshaw and Precious followed euphoric Tango into his house to rehearse the rigged fight.

Back in the Loop, Folks had taken a cab to his hotel suite immediately after Speedy left the gym with the group. Folks and Kid sat in the living room sipping Jack Daniels on the rocks.

Kid said, "Laddie, I think I'll pack and get a flight tonight back to Rita . . . unless you think you'll need me." He drained his glass and stood.

Folks went behind the plexiglass bar to refill his glass. "Pappy, you know how much I appreciate

204

your bringing Tear Off and coming in to help. We won't need you now except to make that phone call tomorrow to the meet suite at two-thirty p.m. as Mister Dolan. The mark won't know if it's local or from Tibet. Pappy, I'll send your ten percent end of the score plus expenses to your hotel in the Apple tomorrow night before we split Chicago."

Folks came from behind the bar, put his arm around Kid's shoulder as he walked him to the door.

Kid said, "Laddie, it's been a pleasure to play with you again. I'm angling to fix Rochester for us, so jingle me at the Sherry Netherlands at least once a week."

They embraced warmly before Kid stepped into the hallway. Folks stood at the open door watching his friend until he disappeared into his suite down the hall.

Folks heard the beat of a drum. Glass in hand, he went to a patio chair and watched a young guy on a hotel patio across the way, practicing on an incredibly shiny, heavily chromed drum. He gazed transfixed, listening to the drum beat as he tried masochistically to snare the infant memories and trauma visions of the past. He felt a ball of tension inflate inside his chest. He fled the patio, went into the bedroom, then shut the door to blot out and forget the sound of the drum across the way.

For some strange reason, he couldn't forget the sound of that drum. He wondered why. He tried to turn his mind from it but it was no use. Then he closed his eyes, surrendered and let his mind grope back through the past. Perhaps it could make some kind of connection there.

Then the painful reason why the sound of that drum was so insistent came in a blinding burst of chrome! On the screen behind his closed eyes he saw once again that glittery, elusive drum . . . .

He saw the featureless image of the blond giant striding through the hazy doorway. He felt again the transient, joyful fear in the pit of his stomach when the shadow had hurled him into the air. He'd catch him and squeeze his cheek against his. At his feet would be the drum.

He heard Phala's, his mother's, cries of happiness as she rushed into the visitor's arms. Then he'd heard her soft, sobbing moans behind her bedroom door.

He saw himself so lonely, amusing himself making faces in the gleaming trim of the drum. He felt a familiar aching boulder of tension roll and tumble inside his chest when he saw himself waking up the next morning. He rushed frantically through the apartment but he couldn't find it anywhere! The drum! That mute, shiny drum was gone again.

Phala tried to blink back her tears. He got in her lap and they bawled together because the drum was gone. One day the drum did come and never came again.

The pictures were becoming more vivid. Spinning on the reel of memory, back to Kansas City, Missouri. It was, perhaps, like the total recall that a dying man might experience.

Shortly after the drum left for the last time, Phala's loneliness and heartbreak became real to him. There were blond white men, many of them, in drunken succession. But no drum. They brought bottles, and far into the night he'd lie awake listening to Phala's wild, sad laughter.

He was a little past three years of age, when his terrible crying seizures started. He'd cry until he threw up. Sometimes Phala would hear him above the clamor of the drunken revelry. She'd come to him in the darkness. He'd be holding his testicles. She'd turn on the light and look. His testicles would be swollen to big sore lumps from his bitter crying.

What a strange thing, he thought, I don't ever remember calling my mother anything except P.G. to her face. The G was for Grisby, her maiden name. She hadn't liked it. She'd begged him to call her mama. She'd threatened, and even tried to bribe him. Finally she gave up.

He remembered her account of how, in 1926, she became a waitress-hostess. She was eighteen years old, had a magnificent body and an Eurasian appearance. Silky clouds of jet hair floated to her twenty inch waist. She'd found it easy to get work in the wooly Roaring Twenties nightspot in Kansas City, Missouri.

Later, in his teens, she told him how she had run away from her home in the country outside of New Orleans. She'd left her father and mother, one sister and four brothers.

Folks remembered his mother told him how she got work as a waitress in a Rampart Street gumbo house. His father and several other white musicians came there one early morning from Bourbon Street. His father was half drunk but he was stricken foolish at the wondrous sight of Phala. He was stone drunk that same week when he actually married his ravishing fourteen-year-old mother.

His father had drummed for three bands by the time he was three. Somehow, despite his drinking, he managed to keep food in their mouths and a roof over their heads. He came to see them only when his band was playing near Kansas City. And when he came, it was usually for only overnight. Then he didn't come at all.

Phala had told him later he had fallen in love with a wealthy white girl and was living common-law with her in the east. But Phala had loved him too much to get a divorce. She always hoped he'd come back to them. He never did!

"Peckerwood cunt, weakling deserter!" Folks said as he left the bedroom.

He went to the bar and poured whiskey into a water glass to the brim and dumped it down his gullet.

Balmy late summer night had fallen when Speedy and Upshaw went to Speedy's hotel suite after a soul food dinner at Tango's house. Dinner had followed exhaustive rehearsal of several ways for Upshaw to lose the rigged fight, which was not to occur.

Upshaw sat in the living room sipping a cool drink, relaxing from the rigors of the rehearsal with Samson. Speedy finished packing his bags in the bedroom. He shoved them into the closet to be scooped up next afternoon after Tango was separated from the hundred grand he was hopping wild to wager on a cinch thing.

Speedy went to the bathroom and pulled out the mirrored cabinet from the wall over the face-bowl. He took his and Folks' bankrolls from the stash, then he extracted twelve grand, in large bills, from his bundle. Chewing his lip thoughtfully, he peeled off two thousand. He shoved the ten grand into his shirt pocket, packed the two grand with the bankrolls into a money belt and strapped it around his waist next to his skin. Then he replaced the cabinet and left the bathroom.

He was going behind the bar in the living room when he heard two light knocks on the door. He looked at Upshaw and dipped his head toward the bedroom. Upshaw went into the bedroom and shut the door.

Speedy put his eye to a peep hole and opened the door to elderly Jake, the bell captain, creased and vivid in his puce monkey suit. Jake went past him as he shut and chained the door. The old man up-ended a brown paper sack and dumped a pile of counterfeit fifties and "C" notes on the coffee table top. Speedy stared down at the phony fortune.

Jake said, "There's a hundred and twenty grand there at ten cents on the buck like I told you. Wanta count it?"

Speedy grinned ruefully. "Jake, I trust your count . . . but, all I could raise is ten grand. Hope you'll split the boodle and still let me cop a hundred grand at ten cents on the buck." Speedy riffled the ten grand.

Jake studied Speedy's poker face with narrowed grifter eyes for a long moment.

Jake shrugged. "Nigger, it looks like you done had a double lucky night since this old scuffler ain't about to stick his ass out copping two grand, wholesale, for twenty gees of sizzling 'queer.' And I sure ain't gonna take it in them streets to pass. 'Course, I'm hip I ain't pulling your coat to nothing you ain't already figured out!"

Speedy slapped the wad of bills into Jake's extended palm. "I owe you two grand, Jake. Now, count it fair and you'll find it there."

Jake said, "Nigger, the bargain you got, it better be right and there," as he shoved the wad into his brown paper bag.

Jake moved to the door as Speedy unchained and opened it. Then Speedy extended his hand. Jake stared at it for a mini instant before he shook Speedy's hand with minimal enthusiasm and went down the hall. Speedy shut the door and Upshaw stepped back into the living room, sat on the sofa watching Speedy stuff the "queer" into a briefcase.

Upshaw said, "I heard Grandpa beefing."

Speedy grinned as he shut the case. "Yeah, he had rocks in his jaw. He'd piss his pants in joy if he knew how close he came to making me a gift of this 'queer'."

Upshaw laughed. "He'd have a stroke, you mean. I wonder why you didn't break his heart."

Speedy shrugged. "He's Folks connected."

210

Upshaw hee-hawed. "Don't drop that lug on me, friend. You know Folks wouldn't turn a blond hair if you ripped off any outside grifter, even if it was his old lady!"

Speedy frowned irritation. "I couldn't be sure that Jake wasn't an exception with Folks. They go back together since he was a punk carny shill."

Upshaw needled, "Come off the shuck. Jake is old and black and you got a sucker soft spot for a mark like that. Always have had in the twelve years I've known you. Right?"

"Right! So you would have taken off Jake. Now, let's get the hell out of here, cold-blooded Tear Off Thomas!"

They stopped off in the ghetto at an auto body-upholstery shop recommended by Precious. In a half hour, the left bottom of the limo's rear seat had a foot and half long section cut out. The aperture from carpet level was concealed by the intact flap of leather upholstery. The next stop was to purchase two identical thick leather valises, with locks and keys, at a Loop luggage shop.

They drove several blocks to a luxury hotel where Folks had rented the Presidential Suite especially to receive Tango and the score the next day. Folks led them through the gem-cut chandeliered entrance hall into the posh gold-leafed living room, sunken and fabulous with richly gleaming furniture and cream-hued brocaded walls and drapes of cobalt blue, shot through with antique gold. They sat down on the blue satin sofa.

Folks lifted a bottle of 1928 Chateau Margaux

from a wheeled cart and filled their glasses. He said, "Here's to the score!" They toasted and drank.

Folks said, "I'm going to order dinner for you guys," as he finger picked and nibbled morsels from the remains of baby quail on the coffee table.

Speedy said, "No, thanks. We let Tango stuff us with garbage soul food."

Folks asked, "We're all set up for the play tomorrow, I take it?"

"All set. The limo back seat is gizmoed, and I copped Jake's hundred and twenty grand in 'queer' and the valises. Tango is creaming his drawers for action. Tonight Upshaw and me will load the dummy valise with paper from the phone book, cut the proper size with the weight of two hundred grand. I'll plant it in the limo switch-nest!"

Upshaw yawned wearily. "I hope we don't make up that boodle tonight, Speedy. I need rest."

Folks stood and stretched, sweeping his arm through the air. "Well, this pad's all yours, pallies. Just sign your name Frederick Dockweider, 111, for food and drink. I'll be back around noon."

Speedy's face was pained as he glanced at his watch. "Partner, it's just ten-fifteen. Don't split with Upshaw sneaking into the land of nod," pointing to Upshaw as his chin dropped to his chest. He snored, fast asleep. "Stay for a couple of hands of gin, two bits a pop."

Folks shook his head as he turned and moved toward the entrance hall. "I got Barbara McNair's double waiting in my bed for a rematch," he said over his shoulder.

Speedy followed him through the entrance hall to the door. "Folks, I got our bankrolls from the stash," he said as he started to unbutton his shirt.

"Leave my bread in your kip until tomorrow," and he opened the door.

"You lucky jockey! A broad that looks like McNair, huh? Where did you cop?"

Folks smiled. "In the lounge at my hotel, couple of hours ago."

Speedy wrung his hands. "Christ, I'm horny for some Big Windy pussy. If I had a nice face and the right paint job, I could slip in that lounge downstairs and con the pants off one of those muckety-muck silk broads laying at the bar."

Folks smiled sadly. Cruel angles of light and shadow deformed his face hideously old and tortured.

"Wade, a white paint job over your blackness could drive you mad. Believe a friend." Folks stepped into the hall and walked away.

Next day, in mid-afternoon, Tango, Samson and the con players were assembled in Folks' Presidential Suite. Upshaw and Samson glared ferociously at each other as per the script. They all sat on the living room sofa and in chairs, silently scrutinizing Speedy, standing, as he counted and stacked Tango's hundred grand wager, in large crisp bills, into the brand new valise on the coffee table.

"A hundred thousand. Correct, gentlemen?" Speedy said.

Tango and Folks nodded.

Speedy started to count Folks' bundle of nearly

perfect phony money. Tango scooted to the edge of the sofa and leaned his eyes close to the coffee table as Speedy audibly counted out Folks' stakes. Speedy packed the bundle into the valise, locked it and tossed the key in his palm.

"Well, whoever is chosen to hold the stakes will have charge of the key," he said as he casually placed the key beside the valise.

Folks said, "Carl, since Mister Dolan is our referee, it seems logical that he should retain the stakes in his office safe until the bout is concluded. That is, if Mister Brice has no objections."

Tango said stoutly, "Mister Hoffman, since we going with your referee, we gotta go with my stakes holder."

Folks said, "Whom would you trust with that responsibility, Mister Brice?"

Tango looked at Speedy. "Carl is going to hold the stakes."

"That's impossible!" Folks said.

"No it ain't, if we bet."

Precious said, "Mister Hoffman, why is it impossible?"

Folks waved his arms in exasperation to explain the obvious. "Because, Carl is my employee. True, he's honest to a fault, but the conflict of interest, with him as stakes holder, compromises Mister Brice unfairly. Let's observe, at least, minimal protocol in this affair."

Speedy said, "He's right, Mister Brice. Looks like Mister Dolan should hold the stakes. He can't judge a fight to the finish, so he's conflict free."

214

Folks said, "I need an aspirin. Excuse me for a moment, gentlemen," as he rose from the sofa and left the room.

Speedy leaned into Tango's face and whispered angrily, "Brother Tango, what the hell you trying to do? Blow the deal?"

Tango answered, "I ain't no fool. Might as well blow the deal now if those two peckerwoods freeze the stakes in that safe with some legal bullshit. Suppose when Upshaw's wind gives out in round twenty-five, like we planned, and Hoffman claims he quit on purpose. Shit, a powerful peckerwood like Hoffman could deny there was a bout, or even that my hundred grand was in the safe. The police gonna take the peckerwood's word. Gambling ain't legal in Illinois, Carl. I'll mash five grand on you. You got to hold the stakes!"

Speedy shook Tango's hand. "Since you put it like that, brother, guess we'll have to convince Junior to let me hold the stakes."

Speedy sat down beside Tango and glanced at his watch. Forty-five seconds before Kid was scheduled to put through the call from New York as Dolan.

Folks entered the room, then seated himself on the sofa. "Well, let's decide on the stakes holder and get to the gym."

Tango said, "We done decided. Carl wants to hold the stakes."

Folks glared at Speedy. "Carl, did you agree to do that against my wishes?"

Speedy sheepishly averted his eyes. "Yes, sir . . .

but only because otherwise, I believe Mister Brice will cancel the bout."

Folks lit a cigarette, puffed it in furious aggravation.

"All right, let's go to the gym. I'll have a word with you later, Carl," Folks said as the phone jangled on the coffee table before him. He picked up the receiver. "Hello Mister Dolan, we were just leaving for the gym." Folks listened for several moments, let disappointment blossom on his face. "Yes, I understand. All right, then you're certain that tomorrow afternoon we can hold the bout? I wish her well. See you then." Folks hung up.

"Gentlemen, the bout is reset until tomorrow afternoon, same time. Mister Dolan's wife's appendix burst two hours ago. He was calling from the hospital." Folks sighed, "I need a drink. How about you, gentlemen?" as he stood and moved toward the bar across the room.

Folks said, over his shoulder, "Carl, perhaps you should give Mister Brice his wager, or take the valise to Mister Sheppard at my bank for safe-keeping in the vault."

The others stood.

Tango stared down at the valise. "Brother, give me my bread so I can lock it up in my own safe. I don't want it outdoors in no peckerwood's vault."

Speedy jabbed an elbow into Tango's ribs. "Dummy up, brother. I'll put all the stakes in your safe," he hissed as he picked up the valise and moved to the bar, followed by the others.

Speedy glanced at his watch. "Mister Hoffman, I better shag to the bank with the valise before it closes."

Folks said, "I'm sure, Carl, the bank vault is the more convenient arrangement for the stakes. I'll see you tomorrow, Mister Brice."

Tango said, "Tomorrow, Mister Hoffman."

Folks glanced at his watch. "Hurry, Carl!" Speedy led the way from the suite and they went to the limo.

Speedy laughed. "Precious, a stakes holder with two hundred grand can't chauffeur. You drive." He gave Precious the ignition key and got in the car on the cushion over the dummy valise beneath him.

As planned, Upshaw let Tango get in the back seat before he got in to crowd himself between Speedy and Tango. Samson got up front with Precious and Precious pulled the limo into heavy Loop traffic. Speedy clasped the valise on his lap, the valise magnetized Tango's darting glances.

Several blocks away, Precious halted the limo at a stoplight. Speedy pointed at a uniformed guard unlocking a closed bank door to let out a customer. They all glanced at the closed bank as Precious pulled away on the green light.

Speedy laughed. "Tango, how could I leave the stakes in Junior's bank vault when it was closed when we got here?"

They all laughed.

Precious said, "And you've got four witnesses!"

They laughed again.

As they neared the Outer Drive, Speedy caught Precious' eyes in the rear view mirror and fluttered an eyelash. Seconds later, Precious shot the limo toward the rear of a truck, then stomped the shrieking brakes. The limo passengers were thrown forward with gut-wrenching violence as the big car haulted inches from the truck.

The dummy valise shot from concealment like a missile, striking the back of Speedy's ankles. He let the valise on his lap slip to the carpet as he hurtled forward with palms thrown against the back of the driver's seat. Then he kicked the cash valise into concealment with the back of his foot as he retrieved the dummy valise from the floor. He leaned back and placed the dummy on his lap as the others recovered.

Precious glanced into the rear view mirror as he pulled around the truck. He stiffened at the sight of a Buick containing four of Tango's hoods in the traffic behind.

17

SHRILL WINDS buffeted the limo and flogged Lake Michigan frothy as Precious drove the Outer Drive toward the southside.

Samson glanced at the speedometer and growled, "Damn, Precious, you doing seventy-five. Lighten up. I nearly went through the windshield in the Loop!"

Precious reduced the speed to sixty. Speedy's bland face concealed the interior ecstasy of the score accomplished. He was unaware that the body shop cutter had electric-sawed into the seat springs and a hanging barb of steel had gouged a half inch puncture into the dummy valise near the top, on the blind side, exposing a flash of printed telephone book boodle.

They reached Tango's house at three-forty-five. Precious parked and they all got out as the four hoods pulled the Buick in behind them and got out.

Speedy said, "Brother Tango, you're the stakes holder until tomorrow," as he gave Tango the valise.

Tango said, "Brother, I sure ain't got the words to thank you for everything."

"You a beautiful brother. It's a pleasure to be in your corner," and he shook Tango's hand.

"How about a drink?"

Speedy's hands shaped a voluptuous pattern in the air. "Got a date, brother."

Tango turned to lead his group up the walkway toward the house.

"Brother Tango, I got us an appointment with a contract expert after the bout tomorrow," Speedy said as he and Upshaw got into the limo's front seat.

Tango made the A-OK circle with thumb and index finger over his shoulder and Speedy goosed the limo away.

Precious went behind the living room bar immediately. Samson, Tango and his four hoods followed to seat themselves on bar stools as Tango placed the black valise on the bar top before him. Precious served Samson ginger ale and the others their choice of whiskey before he served himself a double shot straight, and down the hatch.

Tango's fingertips caressed the valise as he sipped whiskey and dipped his head frenetically to the beat of a disco hit blasting from the bar radio. A laser of late afternoon sun fired through open venetian blinds to illuminate the seat spring puncture in the valise. A corner of printed paper protruded.

Precious was hypnotized as he watched Tango's shocked eyes as he snatched the valise off the bar and tremblingly held it near his face.

Then he leapt to his feet and rammed a finger into the hole as he shouted, "Gimme a knife!"

One of the hoods drew a switchblade, popped it open and gave it to Tango as Tango disemboweled the bag and its paper innards burst forth. Tango made a brutish sound of awful anguish in his throat and sailed the bag to the ceiling, contents fluttering to the carpet.

His face was totally deformed with maniacal rage as he screeched, "Them niggers and that peckerwood done ripped me off!" He turned to the ebonic hood leader. "Boston, we gonna catch 'em and waste 'em. They headed for the Outer Drive back to the peckerwood in the Loop with my hundred grand!"

He flung the door open, braked for an instant and seized the lapels of a bantam hood. "Sparky, didn't you crack, the other day, that you spotted that Carl cocksucker going in a hotel?"

The bantam gasped, "Yeah, offa Forty-seventh Street."

The gang dashed into the street.

Precious went to the window. He watched them get into the Buick and roar away, then he scrambled to the phone and dialed Speedy's southside hotel.

The switchboard woman answered and put him on hold before he could ask for Speedy's suite.

He frantically dialed again. Immediately that he heard the woman's voice, he shouted, "Please!

It's an emergency! Connect me to room four-sixteen."

The woman said, after seeming eons, "Mister Griffin just checked out . . . just a moment."

Precious heard a male voice say, "I think I saw him and his buddy having a drink with Pretty Helen in one of the joints down the street."

He hung up, called Folks and sprinted to the street. He jumped into his jalopy and bombed it away for Speedy's hotel. He spotted the parked limo in the middle of the block at the mouth of an alley. There was a bar at the other end of the block. He braked sharply at the end of the block and coasted into the curb to park, then got out and eye-swept both sides of the block for Tango, in the Buick.

He went down the sidewalk to within yards of the alley mouth when he froze and stared into a record shop plateglass at the alley that reflected the Tango Buick staked out twenty feet up the alley across the street. Then he turned back to his car, got in and was about to "U" turn and go around the block to warn Speedy, in the bar, when he saw Speedy, with valise, and Upshaw leave the bar and come down the sidewalk toward the limo with a high yellow stunner between them.

He hit the middle of the sidewalk and waved his arms as they came forward laughing, with eyes chained to the super fox. He shouted, "Speedy! Watch it! Run!" as they approached the limo.

Speedy's eyes were phosphorescent as he halted and stared at Precious for a long moment. The Buick catapulted into the street and Speedy raced into the alley behind Upshaw. The super fox screamed and fled back toward the bar as the Buick roared into the alley in pursuit.

Precious sobbed as he ran down the crowded sidewalk to the mouth of the alley. He stared into it over the heads of a knot of horrified gawkers as the Buick smashed into Speedy with a terrible crunch sound. He and the valise flew through the air to bowl over Upshaw. The Buick's transmission and brakes howled and squealed as Boston repeatedly backed up and shot the Buick's wheels forward over the prostrate targets, crushed and crimsoned on the alley floor.

Three of the hoods got out and retrieved the valise. Then they stooped over the pair as Boston shot them repeatedly through the head. They tore off Speedy's money belt and rifled their pockets, then almost casually got in the Buick. Boston stomped the Buick into traffic at the other end of the alley.

Precious leaned against a telephone post and vomited until his guts dry-locked. He staggered back to his car and fell inside as an ambulance squealed into the alley. Then he started the car and drove away toward the Loop in a trance.

Folks let him into the suite. "Where are Speedy and Upshaw!?"

Precious stumbled into the living room and crashed limply on the sofa with stricken eyes.

"For Christ sake! What happened!?"

Precious mumbled, "The cruel bastards killed them the dirtiest way . . . ran over them over and

223

over until my heart almost burst. Robbed them! Valise, everything. They had the license plates bent double. I've never been copper-hearted, but they won't get away with it. I'll put the finger on those motherfuckers!" Precious' eyes burst tears as he reached for the phone.

Folks snatched it away. "Get yourself together, Precious!"

Precious leapt to his feet. "I'll make the call to the police somewhere!"

Folks grabbed his shoulders, shook him violently. "Don't crack up like a pussy, Precious!" He flung him back on the sofa.

Precious said, "Gimme some whiskey . . . lots of whiskey."

"Now we're on the same wavelength," Folks said as he went to the bar.

He brought back water glasses and two bottles of Jack Daniels whiskey. He sat down beside Precious and filled the glasses to the brim.

Two days later, at midnight, after arranging with an undertaker to claim and cremate the bodies of Speedy and Upshaw, they checked out. They went to the Eldorado, and Folks pulled it through the light Loop traffic for the highway to L.A.

At a stoplight, Folks gazed at a spectacular blonde beauty crossing before him. For the zillionth time he wondered if Trevor Buckmeister was indeed the most accomplished actor on the planet. He wondered if Christina Buckmeister had been playing castle stink finger, waiting for him when Trevor turned him away.